D1528509

BUTTER WITCH

TORRENT WITCHES COZY MYSTERIES BOOK ONE

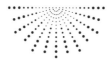

TESS LAKE

TESS LAKE

Shadow Witch

Torrent Witches Box Set #2 (Fabulous Witch, Holiday Witch, Shadow Witch)

Love Witch

Cozy Witch

Lost Witch

Wicked Witch

CHAPTER ONE

"*C*'mon, buddy, I believe in you!"

I whispered sweet nothings to my car as it chugged up the hill, the engine groaning. I could almost hear it talking back to me in every pained rumble.

I'm doing my best, Harlow! I'm a good car! Don't get rid of me!

I switched off the air conditioning and the radio—anything for more power—but we kept slowing. It immediately got warm in the car, but that wasn't unusual. The local weather was more than a little screwy.

It wasn't even a steep hill, and that's what worried me. Nine years ago, I'd bought my car and escaped the city of Harlot Bay—more on that *name* in a moment. A year ago, I'd returned in the same car, for reasons I won't go into right now—let's just say they involved the end of a job, the end of a relationship and a fire—and my car had been with me through thick and thin. In this constantly changing world, it had been my rock.

Now it was at risk of seizing up and becoming a rock on the side of the road. I hoped not. I didn't have the money for repairs or a tow truck. There'd be a lot of walking past it, seeing it sitting dead in the grass every day.

It'd break my heart.

If only magic worked on car engines, but that's not my thing—right now, that is.

We were at a crawl when we made it to the top of the hill. The city of Harlot Bay appeared before me.

Yes, Harlot Bay, North Carolina, a dying seaside town. Once a favorite destination of pirates who arrived for only one reason (ahem), the tiny town grew into a city on the back of commerce, and then it went the other way as commerce went elsewhere. What was once a somewhat thriving seaport is now a confused tourist trap that desperately struggles to stay alive. The townsfolk would do anything to keep it going.

Hence the weeklong International Butter Carving Festival, which was due to start in two days.

Double-hence me, aforementioned *poor townsfolk*, doing anything to survive by running the *Harlot Bay Reader*, an online newspaper/history/recipes/whatever-I-can-think-of website.

Triple-hence me, Harlow Torrent, driving to town to work with a client, and *then* reporting on the council meeting, and *then* helping out my cousins at their store ("help" being a relative term), and *then* probably getting roped into some work at Big Pie, the bakery my mom and her two sisters own.

Yes, Torrent. We were *those* Torrents. The ones the rumors swirled about who lived up the hill in our decrepit mansion. The givers of the evil eye, the wild, wicked women.

The witches.

Nice to meet you. Mwah ha ha, evil cackle, all that.

I drove down the hill, picking up speed as I went. I didn't want too much speed, because frankly, the brakes were shot too, and stopping for a red light needed a lot of advance notice. I'd have fixed them if I had the money, but living in a dying seaside town and having money didn't go together.

So why were the Torrents here? I was here because a year ago, the small publishing company I was working at collapsed in spectacular fashion, due to some light embezzling by the accountant, and we all lost our jobs. My boyfriend at the time, Max, which is short for *complete-stuck-up-shallow-braindead-moron*, decided my sudden bout of unemployment was reason enough to dump me. The night he dumped me, I went to bed crying myself to sleep, with my cat, Adams, by my side. I woke up at midnight to fire alarms and our apartment complex fully ablaze.

Eight apartments burned to the ground. No one was hurt, but everyone lost everything they owned. I was reduced to my laptop, the clothes I was wearing, Adams and my car.

Once the police completed their preliminary investigation and determined it was a wiring fault (it wasn't), I packed my nonexistent bags and drove home.

Home being Harlot Bay. Home being a swirling confluence of magical energy which disrupts the weather in our part of the world—we had snow on the beach once—and attracts witches and other supernaturals and nourishes our souls.

We, the Torrent family, have been here for centuries. The magical energy attracts us, comforts us, and generally makes us feel wonderful and calm.

I'm a Slip witch, so staying calm is especially important.

Enough about witches and magical energy and our dying town. It's my home, I love it most of the time, and my family is here. If my car is a rock, they are my heart.

My annoying, frustrating, bickering, slightly mad, sometimes bad, witchy family.

I hit the bottom of the hill just in time to see my client, John, fling himself off the top of the radio tower that sits smack bang in the middle of town. Down he went, hitting the sidewalk face-first.

I coasted to a stop outside my office space and got out of the car. The engine ticked and cooled. I patted it and promised a servicing in the near future.

As soon as I had some money, of course.

I locked the car and then my heart sank when I saw Hattie Stern striding down the street. *Please, please do not be coming to talk to me about something I've published on my website.*

She marched by, giving me her customary look of disapproval, and continued on her way.

Yes, Hattie, I'm wearing a skirt and calf-high, dark leather boots that look amazing and match my hair and—shut up!

But still: phew.

"She really doesn't like you, does she?"

John had peeled himself up off the sidewalk. I gave a quick glance around to make sure no one was watching. There were enough rumors about our family in town, and appearing to talk to myself in the street certainly wouldn't help matters.

"She hates *us*. Ready for your session?"

John followed me inside.

The *Harlot Bay Reader* had been running for just under a year and had quickly grown to be an important source of news and information for the townsfolk.

Ah, who was I kidding? Sometimes I swore I was the only one who read it, which was sad, given I was the one who wrote it, did the photography, and published it. It was a one-woman show.

I operated out of free office space in a three-story building granted by the city council. In one of the mayor's better ideas—and he had many, many bad ideas—he proposed giving new businesses free office space to operate. It was better than letting the buildings fall into ruin. There were many bored teenagers in Harlot Bay, and some of them vandalized when they got tired of underage drinking. I was the only one in this building at the moment, which was quite handy because, in addition to running the newspaper (without actual paper), I was also working as a post-life resolution therapist.

I made up the title myself. I helped ghosts move on. Well, I was trying to help one particular ghost move on.

John followed me up the stairs and into my office. There was already a fresh twenty-dollar bill sitting on the table. I didn't know where John got them, but he assured me they weren't stolen. He sat down on the battered leather sofa with a sigh.

"That was attempt number three hundred. I thought it might work this time," he told me.

"Hmm." I hummed noncommittally as I pulled out my laptop and got myself settled in. Considering John had told me he was on attempt number three hundred about six months ago and he threw himself off any high place he could find multiple times a week, he was most likely on attempt one thousand or more.

I opened my laptop and brought up my notes.

"This week we're going to go through television shows to see if we can pin you to any specific point in time," I said.

"Oh, I love television! I really like those shows where they have a crime and then the people have to solve it."

About a million shows.

"You've been watching television?"

"Yes, on Mondays I go to Mrs. Tucker's, Tuesdays is the Fergusons', Wednesday through Friday is the McKays' and their huge cinema screen, and then for the weekend, I pop in on whoever looks like they're doing something interesting."

Now it was my turn to sigh. Ghosts and their memories are a tricky thing. Some ghosts are obsessed over one particular thing and can remember it in hyper detail, but they can't tell you their name. Others seem to block out anything painful (like their death). Some, like John, remember general things about their life, but they readily weave in new events. My big plan to reveal that he watched, say, 1970s television, was going to fall in a heap. Back to square one again.

Nevertheless, we started going through the list. He'd paid his twenty bucks and bought his hour, and I was determined to do my best to help him.

The problem with John was that he was John *Smith*. He didn't remember where he lived. He didn't remember children, a wife, parents, a job . . . nothing useful. He remembered going to a baseball game, but he couldn't tell me the teams, the score, or even the weather that day. He didn't know how he'd died. To me, he looked like he was in his midforties, and he was friendly enough, if sometimes a little uptight. We had two sessions per week, and I kept hoping I'd stumble upon something to help him move on. John was hopeful too, but given that I was pretty much the only one who could see or hear him, he didn't have much choice in the matter.

Moving on is another mysterious problem, although it constantly happens.

Why just ghost people? There is ghost *everything*. Grass grows and is cut down, and for a moment there is a ghostly piece of grass. Then it dissipates. I guess grass doesn't have a lot of unfinished business.

I saw a ghost fly once. This fly was coming straight for my sandwich when Adams smacked it right out of the air. Its dead body bounced against the wall. Then a shimmery ghost fly coalesced out of its body, fluttered for a moment, and headed straight for my sandwich again. Adams swiped again but missed. The ghost fly landed on my bread, walked two steps and wisped away, having fulfilled its destiny.

I did not eat that sandwich.

The hour passed quickly, but as usual it was a complete waste of time. He remembered all kinds of shows up to and including what he was watching yesterday. My egg timer buzzed and the session was done.

"Time is up. I'll see you on Thursday."

"Do you think if I stowed away on a rocket going to outer space, I could slip out and maybe throw myself into the sun? Would that kill me?"

"Um . . . I don't know. I know magic, I know ghosts. I don't know about space."

"Oh well."

He walked through the front wall and fell face-first onto the sidewalk below. I quickly packed up my stuff and got out of there. I had what promised to be a very entertaining council meeting to report on.

A ghost in space throwing himself into the sun? I'd have to ask Aunt Cass about that one.

On second thought, I'd see what kind of mood she was in and *then* think about asking her.

No reason to risk getting myself cursed.

CHAPTER TWO

*C*arter Wilkins was glaring at me from the other side of the council chamber. He was the editor, writer, publisher, designer, marketer, and sole owner of the *Harlot Bay Times* (The Only True News Source in Harlot Bay!).

He kept moving his eyebrows up and down as though to really enforce his disdain for me and my website. Each twitch was like Morse code.

Twitch-twitch-twiiiiiitch. Twi-twi-twitch.

I am the only true news in Harlot Bay! You have what? A little "website" on the "Internet"? Who ever heard of such a thing? No one will trust your digital bits as much as my physical paper, girlie.

I focused back on the council members droning away and ignored Carter, but it was truly boring stuff and my mind drifted.

Today was actually one year to the day since I had driven back into town, much to the delight of my family. That meant they were sure to hold some sort of celebration. That meant cake and wine. That meant an extravagant family dinner with a lot of attention on me.

That meant annoyed cousins and an even more annoyed

Great-Aunt Cass, who did not enjoy *not* being the center of attention. That meant acting out.

Yes, we all love each other fiercely, but take triplet witch sisters—my mom, Dalila, Aunt Freya, and Aunt Rohana—who work all day together in their bakery, two witch cousins, Molly and Luce, who work all day together, and Great-Aunt Cass (we usually drop the *Great* because who has time for that?), who is somewhere above eighty and a Slip witch like me who delights in tormenting her family, and you get a very special mixture that could kill you if you weren't careful.

A bickering broth of big-britches witches.

There was no getting out of it, though. It was supposed to be a surprise, but Mom and my aunts had been whispering and giggling that morning in between bickering and sniping, so I knew it was on and there was nothing I could do to get out of it.

The food would be delicious. The company . . . well, let's just say I was glad there was wine served at every meal.

Being that it was the one-year anniversary of my returning to town, it was also almost the one-year anniversary of our guest house burning down and our forced move back into the decaying Torrent Mansion.

I pushed the memory out of my mind. It wasn't my fault. It wasn't my fault.

I tuned back into the councilwoman and back out again just as quickly. The main event wasn't close yet.

Seeing as there's time right now:

Slip Witches.

Hi, my name is Harlow Torrent and I'm a Slip witch.

My cousins are nature witches, my mom and aunts are general all-arounders, and me and Aunt Cass? We're Slips.

Yep, it gets a capital S right there at the start. A Slip witch is one whose powers are pretty much random.

Imagine a roulette wheel on a roller coaster. Spin! What

do we land on today, Chet? (Chet is my imaginary TV show host.) Well, we have garden magic, specifically flowers, and wow, the power is crazy high!

That was a week after my sixteenth birthday. Every flower within two miles of our house bloomed. The ones closest to me got a little snarky and started snapping at people.

Being a Slip witch is awesuck. See what I did there? Awesome and suck together. Bam! Writer! Sometimes I can see the dead as clearly as real people. Other times they're nothing more than a glimmer and a disembodied voice. Sometimes I can kitchen-witch a spectacular roast, vegetables and all. Other times I accidentally turn soup into dirt. Sometimes I start fires in my sleep.

Then there's the whole good witch versus evil witch thing. Actually, it's more like crazy-good-trying-to-save-the-universe-but-causing-a-lot-of-problems witch versus wow-that's-way-way-way-totally-evil-dude witch. Pretty much every mega good/bad witch was/is a Slip. It's like being the really clever kid in your family. The pressure is on to go to college and then do amazing things. At the same time, everyone is just a little worried that you're going to become the mad genius cackling in a lab somewhere, stitching together dead bodies and attempting to hold the sun hostage.

For the record: I am not planning to hold the sun hostage . . . probably.

Why don't I magic up some gold? Yeah, it doesn't work like that.

Back to the droning councilwoman. So there I was in job #3 of many at the time, trying to stay awake. The good stuff was coming—the mayor was waiting to the side, looking like a Japanese punk/cowboy hybrid with an extreme love of hair dye.

Greco Romano is his name, but everyone just calls him

the mayor. He's in his early forties, always seems to be lightly sunburned, and has been mayor for twelve years.

He's totally, absolutely, one hundred percent nutbar.

But he also has this crazy magnetism, so he can bring in crazy ideas and sell them to the citizens. Anything to keep Harlot Bay running and making money. And I do mean *anything*. He once tried to get Harlot Bay branded as "The Spanking Capital of the USA."

Droney McDronerson finished whatever it was she was seeping and then the performance began. Right on cue, about twenty more people turned up to see the fireworks—no, seriously, the mayor once set off fireworks *in the chambers* because he had this crazy idea about Harlot Bay hosting a fireworks festival. The roof caught fire and one of the counselors was "severely singed," according to the *Harlot Bay Times*.

The mayor waved to his assistant, a pale, nervous girl named Elise, and she hit the lights. Complete blackout.

"Sorry."

She fumbled a few times and then a spotlight came up on Greco. He was now in the center of the room in front of us. He leaned over his podium—where the hell did that come from? Did he just drag that in?—and tilted his head down. That week his hair was blond with vivid pink streaks running through it. It was kinda mohawk-y but only on one side. He had a diamond nose piercing that glimmered in the light.

"Butter."

An eyebrow flicker. He moved his gaze across the room, bringing everyone in on his secret. It was working. I leaned forward in my seat, finding myself transfixed. I wanted to know about butter!

He snapped his fingers, a sharp crack that echoed through

the room. Elise got the timing right, and behind him, a huge yellow statue appeared.

It was a man and a woman.

Naked.

Highly detailed.

Amorous.

Made of butter.

"Zero Bend."

Another raspy whisper and a snap of his fingers, and the giant, throbbing . . . butter . . . was replaced with a young guy with spiky black hair and crazy mirror goggles. He was hanging from a harness, upside down, tied to the underside of the Sydney Harbor Bridge in Australia. He was using a chainsaw to carve something out of a massive block of ice that was suspended next to him. Some of the crowd gasped. It was in its early stages, but the emerging statue was even more explicit than the butter guy and girl.

"In two days, Harlot Bay will be hosting the International Butter Carving Festival. Competitors from all over the world will come here to compete for money and fame! With them will come tourists and spectators."

He snapped his fingers again and the spotlight narrowed and brightened until it was just his face.

"Butter," he whispered into the mic.

Then the spotlight winked out. Another moment of darkness and then the lights gently rose up before going too far. The mayor was gone, along with his podium. The council members and everyone else were left squinting in the harsh light. Elise mumbled an apology, fumbled at the buttons, blacked out the room again, and was rescued by one of the junior staffers, who got things working again. She escaped out the side door. As it swung open, I caught a glimpse of the mayor lugging his podium away to his waiting van.

There was a pile of flyers sitting at the front of the room.

Droney banged a gavel like it was a court session and declared the meeting over. I scurried to the front to grab a flyer before Carter Wilkins stole them all—he'd done it before. He took all the flyers on the Great Jelly Riot from last year.

As I left, I saw Hattie Stern pursing her lips at me in the same code Wilkins used. *I get it, Hattie. I'm a lemon, and you don't enjoy the taste of lemon despite running a lemon-based business (Stern Lemons).* Whatever.

She's a witch too. A buttoned-up, clamped-down, iron-corset witch. She's about sixty and does not like me or my family. To her, the Torrent clan is wild, reckless, mischievous, weird, diabolical, crazy, wicked and pretty much all bad.

We take great offense at this characterization.

We're not *all* bad.

CHAPTER THREE

*A*fter lunch and writing a few scintillating articles for my website—a cake recipe, information about a local flower, and a note about the tides—I walked down to Traveler, Molly and Luce's shop. It's a tourist trap in the finest sense of the word. They sell T-shirts, stickers, key rings, bobbleheads of the pirates who used to roam the Atlantic, maps to local attractions, tickets to go out to Truer Island, and basically all of those little knickknacky things that people buy on vacation and then immediately forget about once get home. The thing about Harlot Bay and Hattie Stern was . . . we didn't actually disagree with her about the Harlot Bay name. Unfortunately, it had stuck long ago, been codified (i.e., put on a map), and now everyone was too far down the path to reverse it. Sadly, we had to embrace it. So they had T-shirts that said things like *I went all the way at Harlot Bay*. Hey, we do what we have to do.

If Hattie Stern ever got her way, we'd become Generic Dying Seaside Town #23. At least now we can play on the pirates who sailed the coast, the murders, the ghost stories, the buried treasure and the wicked women who allegedly lived in Harlot Bay.

There are actually quite a few cool things about the place. Some of the houses have tunnels and secret rooms under them, which were used for smuggling and hiding from pirates come to loot everything. They were useful during Prohibition. There are deep caves with gleaming stalactites. Over on Truer Island, there are wild horses descended from Spanish horses who escaped shipwrecks, buried treasure, and a small freshwater lake right in the middle.

I suppose there is the other side of it, though. People stay here for *generations*. Kids you go to school with have the same last names as streets around town. Pick up the paper from 1923 and the town drunk has the same name as today's town drunk. People don't change, the cycle starts anew and we all continue the pattern.

Wow, that was really depressing. I'm sorry. It is a wonderful place, mostly. Promise.

When I got to Traveler, Molly and Luce were arguing, which is the way they are about half the time. They didn't even look up when I walked through the door, the bell jingling.

Molly is short, but don't ever say that to her. She's brunette, a bit curvy like her mom—but *definitely* don't say that to her—and has green eyes that go well with her smatter of freckles.

Luce is taller than Molly and will never let her forget it, with lighter hair than both of us that seems to look blond in one light and tinged with red in another. When she was fifteen, she got a little obsessed about fantasy books and ended up building a life-size catapult, which is kept under a tarp in the woods behind our house. I'm not kidding—an actual catapult.

"No, no, no, you don't start at the Pie Barons and *then* go to the Brewery and *then* go to Hoodoo Voodoo. You have to go in the reverse way and *then* finish at the Pie Barons so you have lunch, and that's the end of the tour," Luce said.

"What are you, crazy? You think people are really going on to the House of Toffee before they've seen the miniature golf course? That's not gonna work. We're trying to make sure they finish at *our* shop with spending money. How about they go this way?"

Molly drew a pen around the map, crossing over many of Harlot Bay's famous landmarks and other associated tourist traps. Luce immediately snorted, took the pen from her and drew an alternate route. I wandered over to the table and they both finally looked up.

"Hey, Harlow, you can settle this. You think you should go to Mr. McGregor's Herbology before or after you've been to Turkey Hut?"

Oh boy, I did not want to get into the middle of this. I hedged my bets.

"Well, I guess that could be a good idea, but I'm sure there's many other great ways to travel around Harlot Bay."

"Chicken," Molly muttered, shooting me a dark look.

"She's not chicken, she just knows an excellent travel plan when she sees it and doesn't want to crush you into the ground right now."

I left the table and flopped down on the sofa that sat against the wall. I was staring out the window, absently listening to Luce and Molly bicker behind me, when I saw a man appear across the street. He was tall, with broad shoulders and wild black hair. Probably a tourist, here today, gone tomorrow. That didn't mean I couldn't enjoy watching him walk around. *Pacing* is the word I'm looking for. He was pacing up and down, and I was very much enjoying his fine form. He was dressed in dark blue jeans and wore a black t-shirt. Scruffy and handsome. Hot, maybe.

Another man joined him who did *not* look scruffy and handsome. He was thin and weaselly looking, with pinched features and thinning red hair. He said something to Scruffy and then passed him something, all the while looking around.

Were they serious? Could you make a drug deal look any *more* obvious?

Weasel Man scurried away. Scruff put whatever it was in his pocket before he looked left and right and then crossed the empty road. Harlot Bay wasn't busy at the best of times; that late in the afternoon you could virtually set up a tent in the main street to sleep in if you wanted. It wasn't until he'd crossed the road and was coming toward the store that I realized I'd been pretty much staring at him the whole way and he had been staring directly at me! I sat up in alarm as he pushed the door to the shop open, the bell jingling. I glanced toward my cousins. Somehow they were still so deep in figuring out the order of their new tour that they ignored the man standing in the doorway.

Whatever part of me had enjoyed watching him run across the street had been absolutely, totally, one hundred percent correct. He was tall and broad, with strong hands and eyes that bordered on blue and green at the same time. He had a light dusting of stubble and a nose that would have looked too dominating on someone else's face, but for him it just seemed to fit perfectly. For the briefest moment, I wondered what it would be like to run my hands through his hair.

What was wrong with me? I had a rule: no drinking before noon. Wait, that's not it. No tourists. It only leads to trouble. But he was handsome . . .

"Are you the owners?" he asked.

Molly and Luce whirled around as one at the sound of his deep voice.

17

"I am," Molly said, jumping forward. Luce joined her approximately point one seconds later, hustling around from behind the counter. I noticed her adjusting her top. Typical.

"Me too—I am owner. I mean I'm *the* owner. One of the owners." She turned red in embarrassment at losing her words. It was unfortunately a family trait around gorgeous men.

"How can we help you?" Molly asked. She pointed at one of the T-shirts. "Did you want to go all the way in Harlot Bay?"

The stranger smiled, his eyes twinkling as a glanced at Luce's red face and Molly standing there with her hand on her hip. He looked across at me and I felt myself involuntarily flush.

"I do want to go all the way in Harlot Bay, but right now I was wondering if you could direct me to the owner of the *Harlot Bay Reader*."

Luce pointed at me.

"Her over there. She one. She is *the* one, she's the one who does it!" She had a finger pointing at me like she was picking a witch out of the crowd, making an accusation rather than being helpful.

I somehow remembered that I had legs—what was wrong with me?—and pulled myself up from the sofa.

"I can help you with that. I'm the owner of the *Harlot Bay Reader*. Harlow Torrent."

"Jack Bishop."

He held out his hand and I shook it. His palm was rough, like he spent a lot of time working with his hands. I let go when I realized I'd been holding on just a moment too long.

"How can I help you, Jack?"

My voice cracked at the end all by itself.

"I wanted to ask you about what your angle was on the

Butter Festival. How are you covering it and all that? Have you dug into the history of all the competitors?"

The truth was that I had hardly done any work at all on it, even though I'd known about it for at least a month. So far I knew famous punk sculptor Zero Bend was coming and they were carving butter, but that was about it. Many years of training in lying to Mom kicked in smoothly.

"I'll be doing backgrounds on all the competitors and then following all the events during the week. Why do you ask?"

"I wanted to know if you'd done any background research on the competitors specifically. Preston Jacobs lived in Harlot Bay about thirty years ago."

"Preston . . . ?"

"He's one of the sponsors of the tour. Made his millions selling plastic buckets and shovels for sandcastle building."

"Why is he important to you?"

"Oh, I'm just interested."

Just interested? He was walking around town looking for the owner of the local newspaper just because he was interested in how they were going to be covering the Butter Festival? Then he happened to be involved in what appeared to be a drug deal? He was lying about something.

"Are you a reporter?" Luce asked.

"That is an excellent question," Jack said, not bothering to answer it. He turned back to me.

Those eyes, my gosh.

He lowered his voice and it felt like he was looking directly into my soul.

"I think you and I should get together . . . ," he said.

My cousins breathed in so sharply my ears almost popped.

". . . if you dig up anything interesting about Preston Jacobs. Here's my card."

He handed me a white card that had Jack Bishop printed on the front and then a phone number on the back.

In my peripheral vision I saw Luce grab Molly's arm. If Jack didn't leave soon, one of them was going to make that *squeee* noise.

"Who was that man you met across the street?" I blurted out.

"Were you watching me?"

"I was looking out the window. It's not my fault *you* happened to walk into where *I* was looking."

I crossed my arms, noticed it was pushing cleavage up, and then dropped them to my sides.

"He's a source."

"So you are a reporter?"

"I'd love to stay, but I have work to do. I'm at the Hardy Arms Hotel."

He turned and smiled at Molly and Luce, who were on the verge of collapsing in an oh-my-heart's-a-flutter.

"Ladies," he said.

Before he walked out, he winked at me.

A wink. At *me*.

The moment he was gone, Luce and Molly let out sighs.

"Oh my gosh, how hot was he?" Molly said.

"Very hot," Luce agreed, fanning herself.

"I'm pretty sure he did a drug deal just across the street," I said. "And he's a tourist."

"Even better. A few nights of passion and then he's gone in the wind," Luce said.

Molly turned to her.

"Oh really, that's what you want? A quick fling with an anonymous tourist?"

"Maybe. I could be interested in that. Why not?"

"Oh yeah, what about William? Have you forgotten all about him?"

There is a somewhat severe lack of good men in Harlot Bay, so a love interest was hot news.

"Who is William?"

"He's nobody. Nothing. Is it time for us to go to dinner yet?"

There was no way I was gonna let this go. I only directly knew two Williams in town—one was the butcher, and he was sixty-five and happily married, and the other one was a statue in the center of town. William somebody, one of the old governors who had actually been somewhat successful in fighting off the pirates who plagued this part of the US. I'm sure he was a good man in his time, but he'd been dead for about two hundred years, and I know Luce doesn't like zombies.

Molly turned to me with a triumphant grin.

"William is a landscape gardener. He is very good with his hands, and in this type of weather he very often takes his shirt off. He is currently working down at the gardens on the restoration project. Luce has been down there three times this week."

"I've just been walking in the park for the sunshine," she protested, turning red again.

"Vitamin D is very important," I said, deadpan.

"I think it is time to close shop. I don't think anyone else is coming today!"

"You want to marry him and have little landscaper babies," Molly teased.

"Oh yeah? You want to explain why you've been spending so much time in the library? A certain new librarian? Perhaps one who looks amazing in a vest? And probably even better out of it?"

Best day ever. Ooh, this was getting juicy. I turned to Molly.

"So who have you been going to see at the library?"

"No one. I've been doing research on . . . pirates. I've been thinking of doing a pirate tour."

"More like thinking of doing a librarian," Luce muttered.

"Is he hunky? Is he one of those guys who looks all nerdy in his vest and his glasses and then suddenly takes his glasses and his vest off and he's fighting bad guys and discovering ancient cursed treasure?"

"I don't know what you're talking about," Molly said. She looked around the store. "I think it's time we closed up. I don't think anyone else is coming. I'm locking up now!"

With that she rushed out to the back room, leaving us laughing.

I collapsed back onto the sofa. What a day full of surprises. *Molly likes a librarian and Luce likes a landscaper and I like a . . . liar.*

What?

I shook my head, trying to dislodge the thought, but Jack Bishop seemed to be stuck in my mind like glue.

No matter. A few days, maybe a week, and he'd be gone and I wouldn't have to worry about him.

I put his card in my pocket anyway.

Luce and I walked back to my office to pick up my car and then drove home, catching up to Molly. The topic of possible new love interests was firmly off the table—at least for the moment, and as long as nobody annoyed anyone else too much. We loved our mothers and aunts, but we had a pact to continue lying to them as much as possible when it came to matters of our love lives. Unless, of course, someone threw you under the bus, in which case you tried to haul them under with you. The last time Molly had mentioned a boy she was interested in, the mothers had gone down to his place of work with a cake that they had also conveniently dosed with a mild love potion! It was too bad it was only a passing attraction—he was a picky eater and refused to have dessert on their one and only date, and who wants to be with a man who doesn't eat dessert? He kept sending her terrible love poetry for the next few weeks until the potion wore off.

He sent her:

I'm blue
because I'm not with you
and I don't know what to do

Our Aunt Cass read it and suggested he go *ride a kangaroo* until he came to his senses.

We drove up the hill, the sun rushing down to the horizon behind us. The fading light lit up Torrent Mansion, hiding its flaws from view.

The mansion is gigantic, with a stupid number of rooms, three stories up and at least two stories underground. It was built a long time ago, and every generation of Torrent witches had added their own touch. Molly, Luce and I lived in what you'd technically call the East Wing.

You think mansion and you think wealth, right? Old money, servants to clean all the windows, perhaps even a butler.

The Torrent Mansion is falling to pieces. The floorboards are old, there is water damage, and we can't actually walk from our end of the house to the middle because the floors aren't safe. The mansion started falling apart decades ago, so my great-grandmother's family built a new guest house on the property that simply became *the house* after a while. With a severe lack of funds to rebuild the mansion, they just moved out. We were all living in the guest house up to a year ago, and . . .

I took a deep breath as we pulled up to our front door, feeling a sudden prickle of tears.

It wasn't my fault. A sleepwalker isn't responsible for what they do, and neither is a Slip witch. It was a little hard to convince myself even now. A fire had sent me back home, and there had been another only a few days after I'd returned.

After the fire, our mothers had gone deep into debt to renovate the middle of the mansion, where they lived along with Aunt Cass, and the East Wing, where Luce, Molly and I lived.

We stopped out front and let ourselves in. The main entrance leads to stairs, which are unsafe, the dining room, which is renovated and okay, and the kitchen, which is the heart of the house.

Bickering voices rose up from that direction.

"Oh boy," Luce said.

"Get in, get out, it will all be okay," Molly said.

We could all hear Aunt Cass's raised voice. The chances of it all being *okay* were not good.

We went in through the dining room and into the kitchen.

"What's happening, family?" I asked.

"Nothing," Aunt Cass snapped.

I glanced at mom and my two aunts. They were all busy cooking or pretending to fuss around. Molly and Luce took up spots near their respective mothers.

The family:

Aunt Cass is short and wrinkled, somewhere over eighty, and takes special pleasure in tormenting her family. Imagine a lemon that someone left out in the sun so it dried up like a sultana, and then give that lemon magical powers and an attitude you couldn't knock over with a bulldozer.

My mom, Aunt Freya and Aunt Ro are nonidentical triplets in their fifties. My mom is blonde with blue eyes and seriously looks like she should be on a Scandinavian cereal box or something. She even has red cheeks! She is also the tallest of the sisters—another gene that missed me. Freya has dark hair and dark eyes much like me, is in the middle for height, and is somewhat curvier than both her sisters, though not by much—they run a bakery and delight in sampling their own product. Ro is the shortest sister and also the youngest by about three minutes. She has pitch-black hair and a slightly olive complexion, a gene that missed Molly by a country mile.

The main words that should spring to mind are *bustling* and *busybodies*.

We love them, but sometimes . . . ugh, it's too much. Still, we never miss the opportunity for a little stirring.

"Why the raised voices?"

"I caught her giving a haunted ghost tour through the mansion this afternoon," Mom said.

Aunt Cass snorted.

"*Caught* me? You can't *catch me* doing something in my own house! What's next? You're going to *catch me* making a piece of toast?"

"One of the tourists fell through the floor. Luckily there was a very old bed in the room below."

"He's fine. It was exciting for them."

"He nearly broke his leg. If that bed hadn't been there—"

"Money is money, and I need to make a living now that the Feds have shut me down," Aunt Cass said, crossing her arms.

Mom shook her head behind Aunt Cass's back and continued chopping tomatoes.

I knew this wasn't a good idea, but I couldn't help myself.

"The Feds?"

"The man, Uncle Sam, the *government* that has nothing better to do than to stomp on the small businesswomen."

"How did they stomp on you?"

"They shut down my online healing shop!"

"They were placebos," Mom blurted out.

"If they work, they're not placebos."

25

With that, Aunt Cass stormed out of the kitchen. Mom waited until her footsteps had faded.

"She was selling sugar pills to treat certain . . . male conditions," she whispered.

Ah, right. Suddenly a lot of things fell into place. About a month back, Aunt Cass had started insisting on being taken to town with us when we went to work. Normally she stayed at home. We'd drop her off at the post office and then pick her up at the library. No doubt she'd been using their computers to run her burgeoning drug empire.

"She even had a website," Ro whispered.

"What was it?"

"I can't tell you," she replied quickly.

"Why not?"

"Forget it, it's closed down now," Mom said.

"I want to know what it was called!"

"It had some very suggestive words in it. That's the end of it. We're not discussing it."

She pointed her finger at me. "Don't you bring it up with her. Oh, and tell your cat to stay out of our pizza oven. He was in there again today."

I raised my hands in protest.

"I'm not his boss. I can ask him to stay out, but he does his own thing."

"The day a customer gets cat hair on his pizza, then maybe you'll take it seriously. He's downstairs, go tell him now while we get dinner ready. That pizza oven is helping keep our family afloat. Do you want to bankrupt us?"

Ouch, that turned quickly.

"You two scoot out of here and stop stealing food," she added, pointing her knife at my cousins, who were, in fact, stealing food at that very moment.

"We're not stealing food!" Molly protested through a mouthful of croutons.

I trotted off downstairs to say hi to Grandma before the battle hit me.

Grandma is April Torrent, Aunt Cass's twin sister and my mom and aunts' mother. Adams was curled up at her feet. He stood up and yawned, showing me a mouthful of sharp white teeth.

"Is it dinner yet?" he asked.

I picked him up and he snuggled into me. He smelled like pizza.

"Good to see you too, Adams. I had a wonderful day, thanks for asking," I said.

"Mmf," Adams said, starting to purr.

"Why do you smell like pizza?" I asked, although I already knew the answer.

"I don't know."

A month ago, my mom and aunts had a pizza oven installed at Big Pie. It was a somewhat costly improvement that allowed them to add pizzas to their menu. It was also Adams's new favorite place to sleep.

Not behind it, on top of it, or near it, an adorable little black cat basking in the warmth.

Nope, Adams preferred *inside it*, up the back. The thing ran at a few hundred degrees, and he'd be in there snoring away.

"Please try to stay out of the pizza oven when they're making food for customers."

"Mmf," Adams said, rubbing his head against me.

I carried him over to Grandma.

My grandma April is Cass's identical twin, except she is frozen in time. She looks to be in her sixties, whereas Aunt Cass is now in her eighties. It won't be long before our moms will look the same age as her.

She has been frozen since I was seven—twenty years ago now. My memories from back then are all a bit of a blur, but

I remember she was kind and loving, certainly nothing like her sister. She always had a cookie somewhere and would sweep us up in these big hugs.

She's still alive but . . . frozen. A living statue. She has her hands out in front of her like she's holding an invisible basketball and has a look of intense concentration on her face with just the hint of a smile like she's happy with whatever she's doing. Only Aunt Cass knows what happened to her, and the only thing she ever says about it is that Grandma bit off more than she could chew.

Not surprising for a Torrent witch. Biting off more than we can chew is practically our family motto.

Actually, she does say something else. We can't undo what has been done, so don't bother trying.

"Hey, Grandma, how are you today?" I asked. "Oh, that's good. Me? Just a normal day. Still working with John and reporting. The Butter Festival is on this week . . ."

I told her about what I'd been doing, receiving only comforting silence in reply. Our whole family does it—comes down here to chat and spill our hearts out to her. Sometimes even Aunt Cass comes down and locks the door to spend some private time with her frozen sister.

It wasn't long before Adams got tired of my holding him —typical finicky cat—and fidgeted for me to let him go. Soon after that, Mom called down the stairs that dinner was ready.

I took a deep breath and looked at Grandma.

"Well, let's get this fiasco started," I said.

CHAPTER FOUR

*D*inner at the Torrent Mansion is not so much a meal with good conversation as food served alongside a free-for-all verbal sparring tournament as seven witches poke, prod, snark, mock and generally dig their noses into everyone else's business.

I could practically hear the announcer as I walked up the stairs.

"In the red corner with oh so many wins, most obtained by sneaky, underhanded moves and very few losses, is Aunt Caaaaaassss! Her special move is: Strike Fear! In three separate corners we have Ro, Freya and Dalila, who will be tag-teaming tonight using moves such as Don't Argue With Your Mother, I Told You So, and the always popular Divide and Conquer! Entering the ring now, with no corner to stand in, are Molly, Luce and Harlow. Special moves include Working as a Team Until You Annoy Me, The Lie Sandwich (lie, tiny bit of truth, lie) and Oh I'm Sleepy Need to Go to Bed. How will the battle go tonight, folks? It's sure to be bloody!"

I was the last to arrive in the dining room, which is usually not the position you want to be. In the middle of the room is a beautiful large, polished oak dining table that is about as old as the house. It's big, heavy and wide, which is actually quite handy when someone attempts to lunge across it. It's too far to make it across easily—not that it ever stopped anyone from trying.

We usually cluster down on one end. Aunt Cass sits at the head of the table, the moms on one side and Luce, Molly and I the other. Whoever turns up last has to sit near Aunt Cass and is assigned the role of partially being her handler and partially being her first target. When I walked in, Luce was in that position, rubbing an angry red mark on her arm with a pained expression. Molly quickly patted the chair that sat between them. Evidently, they'd saved the middle seat for me —being that it was my unofficial one-year celebration—but then had to fight it out as to who sat next to Aunt Cass. Clearly, Molly and her superior pinching prowess had won.

"Oh, you're here. I thought I was going to starve to death," Aunt Cass said.

Unofficial celebration or not, she wasn't going to let anything change the way she treated us.

I ignored her and took my seat. Spread out before me was a selection of my favorite foods. There was a gigantic pan of lasagna with a crisp, cheesy top, and next to it was a bowl of leafy green salad. On the side there were cheesy, bacon-smothered potatoes, garlic croutons, and a mixed assortment of roasted root vegetables. Delicious cheesy carbs served with a side of carbs and accompanied by more carbs. I silently sent my apologies to my thighs. I saw that Molly had already poured us glasses of red wine, and the moms had stocked up too. Aunt Cass had a bottle to herself.

We served ourselves, quickly filling our plates. This was the calmest part of the meal, before the real show began. I'd just put a piece of delicious lasagna in my mouth when Ro fired off the first salvo.

"So, how is Traveler going this week?"

"It's fine," Molly said quickly. She picked up a glass of red wine and took a gulp.

"Making plenty of sales?"

"About in line with this time of year," Molly said. She took another gulp of wine.

"I saw a very good coffee machine online—high-quality and makes incredible espressos and cappuccinos. They even send you a book written by an Australian barista, and you know they're the best. I was thinking it might be good for Traveler. Sell someone a coffee while they're buying fridge magnets and T-shirts. Maybe get a cold drink fridge as well?"

"We are fine with the business how it is," Molly said. She viciously stabbed her lasagna.

Traveler and its success or lack thereof was somewhat of a touchy subject with Molly and Luce. Just like me, they were operating their business rent-free thanks to the mayor's initiative. If they had to pay rent, their business wouldn't survive. Not that Big Pie Bakery was a roaring success, but the moms made just enough money to keep us all afloat, so that translated into them being business geniuses who could liberally give out advice on anything. The thing was . . . a coffee machine wasn't such a bad idea. Tourists who came to Traveler had often just arrived in town or were about to leave. In either case, a hot cup of coffee or a cold drink would probably sell well.

So why was Molly resisting it? *General principle.* If Ro was right about this, then perhaps she was right about lots of other things too. You never wanted to give a meddling mother any more ammunition than she already had.

"I don't want to serve coffee or cakes or cookies. It's not a cafe. It's a tourist shop. I'm happy with the way it is."

"I agree with her. A small businesswoman should be allowed to run her business in whatever way she sees fit,"

Aunt Cass said, very pointedly looking at the moms. She was clearly still annoyed that her growing drug empire had been shut down.

I took a gulp of red wine and it must have gone instantly to my head.

"Do you have any ideas of something else they should sell in that shop?"

"What you mean?"

"Oh, I don't know. Perhaps there are other products that would be good to sell to tourists, perhaps who are coming to Harlot Bay to have a good time . . ."

Aunt Cass pointed a finger at me. "Don't think I don't know what you're doing, young lady."

The instant flood of alcohol vanished, leaving just the sound of me digging my own grave. It wasn't a good idea to pick on Aunt Cass. She didn't worry too much about the general opposition witches had to cursing other witches. In fact, she considered cursing just another way to make sure people respected her and also to get her own way.

"Yes, what do you mean?" Mom said, giving me a glare.

Oh no. Had I suffered a head injury of some type? What kind of fool threw themselves into the deep end in the first five minutes of dinner? I panicked.

"There's a new librarian in town. He is very cute."

Molly and Luce turned to me, both their faces pale. Was I insane to bring up possible romantic partners? Maybe, but I didn't want to get blamed for starting a conversation about placebos and the male conditions they were supposed to solve. The moms leapt on the news of a new handsome librarian like lionesses taking down an antelope.

"Is he single?" Ro asked.

"Have you talked to him?" Freya said.

"I haven't met him; Molly mentioned him today."

"I did not! Luce was the one who started talking about

him, and that's only because I was teasing her about the landscape gardener she is in love with, which only happened because we were teasing you about the tall, scruffy and dangerous man who came into the shop today."

Molly put a hand over her mouth as if in a desperate attempt to literally hold her lips shut and stop spilling all our secrets.

"A landscape gardener? What landscape gardener? Where does he work?" Ro asked.

"Who was this boy who came into the shop today? What do you mean he's scruffy and dangerous?" Mom said.

"There are no boys, there is no one; we're not having this conversation, our love lives are out of bounds." Luce waved her hands as though to push the conversation away from us, but the jackals on the other side of the table weren't so easily dissuaded.

"I'm never going to get grandchildren," Mom said.

"Probably die alone," Ro added.

"These are your best years. You need to find a man before your looks go, which isn't that far away," Freya said, looking us up and down.

"Pish posh! There's plenty of time for them to get pregnant and have babies. What we need first in this family is economic security, and the only way we're going to get that is if we allow the entrepreneur, the small businesswoman, to make a go at it."

Aunt Cass thumped a fist on the table. We all knew a lifeline when we saw it, even if it was one that would possibly lead to conversations we really didn't want to have with our mothers and very elderly aunt.

"That's a great idea, Aunt Cass," Luce said. "What kind of business where you thinking of running?"

"I heard you snickering before, missy, so don't think you can sweet-talk me now by pretending to be on my side." Luce looked at her plate as though it was suddenly the most interesting thing in the room.

"I want to know about these boys," Mom said.

"It is very important to run a good business," I said, trying to cool things off and change the topic.

"Oh, is it? You have a spelling mistake on your website. You left a letter off a word," Aunt Cass said.

She's reading my Harlot Bay Reader *website?*

"Where?"

"I'm not being paid to be your editor."

I looked down at my food and focused on getting as much of it into my mouth as I could, as fast as possible. There probably was no mistake and she was just sending me off on a wild goose chase for her own amusement. Still, it had gotten us off the topic of any men we might be interested in, although I knew our mothers wouldn't forget it. I also knew that as soon as we got out of there, Molly and Luce were probably going to kill me for even bringing it up.

Right at that moment, I felt Adams rub himself against my leg. Before I could even reach to break off a piece of cheesy crust from the lasagna to feed him, Mom snapped, "No feeding the cat under the table."

"Who made that rule?" Adams said from somewhere near my feet.

"Stop getting inside the pizza oven."

I heard Adams grumble something, and he wandered further up the table to sit under Aunt Cass's chair. With Mom watching, Aunt Cass very deliberately cut off a piece of her lasagna, took it off her plate with their fingers, and put her hand under the dinner table. She stared at Mom, daring her to say something.

"Cats shouldn't eat human food," Mom finally said, looking away first. By this time we had finished our main course, which meant we only had dessert to get through before we could bail out of there.

Mom picked up her half-full glass of wine. She took a gulp before raising the rest of it up into the air.

"Tonight is one year since Harlow returned to us. We're so delighted you came home, darling. Because this is what family means. They stay together and treat each other with respect. Cheers."

We all lifted our glasses and mumbled cheers. You could practically hear everyone's sarcastic remarks crackling in the air. There was Mom's dig at our absent fathers, who were all long gone. And respect? Was that the same as sticking your nose into everything?

With the main meal over, Mom, Ro and Freya quickly gathered up the plates and took them away.

While they were gone, Molly whispered to me, "You are so dead." She pinched me on the arm.

"Ow, leave me alone. That hurts."

"Why did you snitch on us?" Luce whispered from the other side. She didn't pinch me, but she had a crazy look in her eye that suggested she might do something else.

"I didn't snitch, I just thought it would be interesting dinner conversation."

"Snitch," Molly said. She tried to pinch me again, but I smacked her hand away.

"Stop it. You need to protect each other. Stop fighting," Aunt Cass commanded.

"She snitched on us," Molly said.

"So what? The three of you have been snitches ever since you said your first words. Tattletales who snitch on family to save your own skin. It's about time you learned a little something about being there for your family and keeping their secrets."

This didn't sound good.

"We're not snitches," Molly protested.

"Oh no? I wonder how it was that your mothers found out about my online business. Were they perhaps searching for some male erection treatments? Did they happen to stumble upon it and then order some treatments and discover that I was the one who was sending them? Or did someone who is a snitch somehow figure out what I was doing and tell them?"

Aunt Cass's every sentence dripped with sarcasm. She looked from Molly to Luce and back again.

"I don't know what you're talking about," Luce said. When in trouble, it was best to deny everything. She might still get you for it, but if there was something Aunt Cass admired, it was a good lie.

So Molly and Luce had evidently been the ones to uncover Aunt Cass's drug empire. I'd have to ask about that after dinner and perhaps keep it as ammunition for when they came after me for revealing the men they were interested in.

"Dessert!" Mom announced. Ro pushed the door open and Freya came through with a bowl of whipped cream.

Mom carried in our mansion in cake form on a giant silver platter.

It was spectacular. It wasn't our mansion as it was at the moment—dilapidated, falling down around our ears, and liable to collapse at any moment. It was restored, beautiful and new.

Our mothers are amazing witches, but they especially have an affinity for cooking and kitchen witchery. Every year they enter into cake competitions, pie competitions and generally any cooking challenge where they can compete against each other. The three of them are so good that the competition organizers often have to award joint first place.

"Wow," I breathed, looking at the cake. I didn't know how they'd managed to keep this a secret.

"We have some news," Freya began.

"What news?" Aunt Cass demanded.

The three older women shared *the look*. We all knew it well. It was the *we have something to tell you, but you're probably going to go crazy, so we're going to try to do it very gently, but please don't go crazy* look. With Aunt Cass already worked up about the end of her business, they'd have to tread carefully.

"Well, Big Pie is going well enough that we've been able to get a little bit of money out of it. We're thinking of transforming this place into a bed-and-breakfast that we're going to call Torrent Mansion," Mom said.

There was a moment of silence as we digested this news.

"How are you going to make this into a bed-and-breakfast? There are about a million rooms and the whole place is falling apart. Did someone die and we inherited a lot of money that I don't know about?" Molly asked.

"Don't be sarcastic. This town definitely needs good business development," Ro snapped.

"We're going to build from the center out. We've already renovated this part, and we can do the rooms around it and block off the rest of the house. As we make money, we can continue to expand until the entire mansion has been renovated from top to bottom."

"But what about Grandma?" Luce asked. "And what about all the other witchy things around this place? You want to have workmen in here seeing the hex symbol carvings in that bottom room?"

"What about that weird feeling you get down in the other end of the house that might be some kind of spirit?" Molly added.

"It's fine. We can move your grandmother and keep her safe. Besides, most of the workmen know about our family stories already, so it's not any surprise for them if they find some strange carvings or markings on the wall. We might play on it, a sort of witch-based bed-and-breakfast. Guests will find it charming," Freya said.

"Or find a dead body buried under the floorboards," Molly muttered under her breath. We all looked at Aunt Cass, waiting to see what she would say. She rarely takes news well. She seems to believe that the moment you know something, she should know *immediately* or you should have discussed it beforehand with her, and of course you were trying to spring it on her just so you would get your own way.

"What are you looking at me like that for? I think it's a good idea. This place has been falling down for years, and if the bakery is making enough money to renovate, then we should."

This was certainly a new development. Normally Aunt Cass would kick up a big stink about something, which was generally a ploy just so she could get her own way on something else. I was surprised they'd spring something this big on her, honestly. On the other hand, they probably didn't want to give her time to think up a long list of demands.

"Is the bakery really making that much money?" I asked.

"It's making enough money that we can get a loan against it. We can use that loan to renovate enough of the mansion for us to open a bed-and-breakfast and block off the rest. We're going to advertise it as a historical heirloom coming back to life. There are a lot of people who are very interested in old houses."

"There were a lot of people interested in taking ghost tours through old houses too until you shut me down," Aunt Cass said.

"We can discuss ghost tours if you want," Mom said diplomatically.

I took a quick photo of the cake mansion with my phone and then Ro cut into it. Inside, it was a chocolate-and-vanilla marble cake with a chocolate filling that ran through it in stripes. It was absolutely delicious, and for a short while there was mostly the sound of seven witches eating and not sniping at each other.

I wasn't sure how I felt about this new idea. One thing Harlot Bay is known for, at least locally, is all the businesses that open and then shut down within six months to a year. It's basically a plague. Someone, usually not from here, has the idea of opening up a shop on the seaside that, say, sells flowers, and they don't understand the realities of running a business in a tourist town. The mayor's initiative helps by giving free rent, but that really just seems to increase the number of failing businesses. Honestly, the ones that succeed are always weird. I assume it's the magical conflu-ence in this area and the strange people it attracts. They don't start normal businesses. It's pretty odd, actually. There is a Viking-themed bar called Valhalla Viking that is success-ful, and so virtually every year someone tries to open a pirate-themed bar. You'd think it would succeed given all the crazy pirate activity up and down the coast in the past. But inevitably, people go to Valhalla Viking and the pirate bar closes down until someone else comes along to try again.

There were already bed-and-breakfasts in Harlot Bay, but there was definitely nothing like Torrent Mansion. I could see where there might be some attraction to it, although I didn't know who would want to stay overnight at a place that would be constantly undergoing renovations. Taking a loan out against the bakery didn't sound like such a great idea. We were barely hanging on as it was, and too much debt could go bad very quickly.

I gulped down my cake and refilled my glass of wine,

topping up Molly and Luce also. I noticed that Aunt Cass was most of the way through her bottle herself.

I shook the negative thoughts out of my head. While the Torrent family is wild and sometimes crazy, and has possibly been wicked in the past and on other occasions, we also don't give up. Every one of us was trying as hard as we could to pull our entire family out of the borderline poverty we'd fallen into. Maybe this would be just the thing to turn our fortunes around. I raised my glass in the air.

"To new endeavors!" We clinked our glasses together and drank.

Then we got out of there as fast as we could and rushed back to our end of the mansion, Adams trotting along behind us. Luce and Molly seemed to have forgotten my hauling our possible romantic lives out at dinner in the face of the threat of Aunt Cass blaming them for Dalila, Ro and Freya discovering and subsequently shutting down her online business.

"She blames us! She's gonna curse us, I just know it."

"We drive through the night and by morning, we're Canadian," Molly said.

"I love maple syrup," Luce said.

"No, we go *south* and cross into Mexico. She'll never find us."

"Ooh, guacamole!"

Molly turned on Luce. "What is it with you and food right now? Are you pregnant or something?"

"For me to be pregnant, I'd have to . . . shut up."

"Why does Aunt Cass think you snitched on her?"

Molly raised a hand to her forehead—perhaps wiping away panic sweat or maybe checking for warts or goat horns that were going to erupt at any moment.

"Mom had something strange on her credit card and wanted to know if it was me. It was a shipping company charging small amounts of money to her. I asked Luce, and she checked Freya's statement and found similar charges. We told them to dispute them with the bank and then it turned out it was Aunt Cass buying supplies online! She thinks we snitched on her!"

As Molly said *snitched* she suddenly remembered my traitorous behavior at dinner.

"You! What are you, mental? Those witches are going to be out looking for every librarian and landscape gardener in town now! I'm going to get you for that."

I rubbed my arm, pretending it hurt a lot more than it did.

"You already got me. Besides, I outed myself too."

"Oh, so you do like Mr. Tall, Dark and Touristy?"

"Um, no, I mean . . . just that they'll be picking on me. I don't like him."

"Yes, you do," Luce and Molly teased in unison.

"You want some of that scruffy tourist coming through town. Here today, gone tomorrow, no names, just a night of passion," Molly said.

"I do not!"

"I really enjoy not falling over," Luce said.

Years ago, when Aunt Cass suspected the three of us of stealing her wine, she'd cursed us with being clumsy for a good three months until we came clean. We could hardly walk more than three steps down the block without falling over, banging our elbows and knees, or bruising ourselves on low tree branches. It got so bad that the school nurse suspected we were all being beaten at home. Only when we confessed to Aunt Cass did the curse lift—although she denied she'd ever cursed us in the first place and insisted we were all simply clumsy.

"If I fall over because that old lady curses me, it's gonna be war," Molly said.

Luce put her hands on her hips. "Oh please, what are you going to do to her?"

"I don't know, but it's going to be effective. She's the one committing credit card fraud, and we end up cursed because she gets caught? What are we supposed to do, check with her first if we discover a crime in progress? Make sure she's not involved?"

"Wouldn't be a bad idea," I said. Aunt Cass considered the law a loose set of guidelines when it came to her—unless she was trying to use it against you, in which case they were iron.

"I have to go to bed. I start reporting on the Butter Festival tomorrow," I said with a yawn.

"I only just got my eyebrows back," Luce said, brushing her fingers across them.

I left Molly and Luce plotting revenge in the kitchen and took myself off to bed. Adams curled himself up at the foot of my bed. A year ago minus one day, I'd gone to bed with him sleeping at my feet and we'd been awoken by fire alarms. Thankfully, that hadn't come up at dinner. Last time I'd talked about it, Aunt Cass had whacked me with her cane that she sometimes carried (mostly when she was trying to get out of something using the "I'm Old" excuse) and told me it wasn't my fault and to stop being such a "moany moaner."

As I drifted off to sleep, the past and present mixed together. My ex-boyfriend appeared, and just as I was about to kiss him, he transformed into the handsome stranger. I tried to push him out of my mind, but to no avail.

He was a tourist, and I didn't get involved with tourists, I told myself.

CHAPTER FIVE

*T*he next morning I got up and had a very quick breakfast while Luce and Molly very sleepily discussed the idea of getting a coffee machine for Traveler. They'd obviously stayed up late fretting over what Aunt Cass might do to them or plotting revenge for when she did do whatever she was going to do. I got out of there before they could wake up too much and remember I had thrown their romantic lives out onto the table. I patted Adams and headed out the door.

I drove to work and got there just at eight o'clock. When you're self-employed, it's very important that you treat your job as though it were a *real* job, as though there is a boss watching you come and go. Otherwise, it's very easy to start sleeping late and leaving early, and pretty soon you're only working maybe one hour a day. I honestly had no idea if the *Harlot Bay Reader* was ever going to become successful enough to pay me like a regular business, but I was trying as hard as I could to make it so. The problem with Harlot Bay is not very much happens here. Sure, there are crimes, and the magical confluence in the area certainly causes a few weird things to hit the front page, but it's hardly enough to sustain everyone's interest and certainly not enough to generate advertising dollars.

I walked up the steps to my office and went inside and up the stairs. John was sitting on the sofa watching the television. Two very excited, tanned people were discussing the benefits of a truly amazing blender that could make fruit juices in under half a second.

"Hey, John," I said, making myself a quick coffee and gulping it down.

"Good morning. Did you know you can get this blender for only three easy payments of $59.95?"

"Is it a good deal?"

"Of course it is. This blender has eighty-five separate functions."

"Sounds nice," I said, thinking about other things.

"Are you going to be reporting on the graffiti?"

That caught my attention. Graffiti?

"What graffiti are you talking about?"

"Someone sprayed paint on the front of a few shops this morning. Unbelievable."

"I'll check it out," I said, shuffling through my papers. I finally found the Butter Festival flyer that I'd picked up at yesterday's council meeting.

"Okay, gotta go out, see you later," I said, checking that my camera battery was fully charged.

"It does crinkle-cut potato chips. Can you believe it?" John said, his attention back on the television.

I left him there, watching the marvels of modern engineering, and walked down the street heading for the town hall where the Butter Festival would take place. As I walked along I browsed through the flyer. There were a series of competition butter carvings running through the week and also some display events. The lead competitor, Zero Bend, was scheduled to do an ice carving at the Festival's Grand Opening later today. There was a photo next to his name. He had spiky punk hair, dyed black, pink, green and red, which stuck out everywhere. He was wearing a thick pair of black goggles and had a snarl on his face. Black tattooed lines crept up his neck. The small bio about him called him "the bad boy of sculpture." Below him was Holt Everand, his closest competitor. He wasn't as punk looking as Zero Bend, but he did look just as crazy, with spiky blond hair so light it practically glowed. There were a few more competitors who'd be there, all with weird names. Harmonious Twang. The Slice. Jim Fire. It was all proudly sponsored by Preston Jacobs, referred to as the Sandcastle King.

I was so caught up in reading that I didn't see the bunch of adorable six-year-olds walking by under the supervision of their teacher until I nearly stepped on them. It wasn't cold at all but some of them were rugged up like it was snow season. Maybe they were going to our very old and falling-apart ice-skating rink, Cold Blades.

Zero Bend's name rang a bell. I couldn't remember what, exactly, but I was pretty sure he had gotten arrested in some country for doing something stupid and crazy. One of those things that gets about two seconds on the news at the end when they need to say something light-hearted like "Crazy Artist Arrested for Stealing Elephant."

I stuffed the flyer back in my pocket and continued on down the street past the town hall to the grouping of ware-houses they were using to store the tons of butter for the competition. I was expecting someone to be here to let me in to take some photos for the *Harlot Bay Reader*, but the place was deserted. I knocked on the front door, but no one answered, so I went walking around the side until I found another door that was ajar. I knocked on it and it pushed open under my fist.

I stepped inside, feeling a cool wash of air over me.

"Hello? Harlow Torrent from the *Harlot Bay Reader*—I'm here to take photos."

My voice echoed out into the corridor and the room beyond. There didn't seem to be anyone around. I walked down the corridor, looking into the rooms on either side as I went, but they were empty.

I pushed through the plastic flaps into the main chill room. It was kept at near freezing in there, and my breath plumed out in front of me. I quickly removed my camera lens so it would have time to adjust to the temperature. The tables all around me were filled with giant wrapped pats of butter. Each one must have been at least twenty pounds. I wasn't one to waste a good opportunity, so I went over to the nearest table, knelt down, and started taking photographs.

I moved around, trying to find a good angle to include the butter brand and the size of it. Every shelf around me was filled with thousands upon thousands of pounds of butter. This was at least going to make a great article. Hopefully I had better pictures and copy than Carter Wilkins.

I wandered around the room, feeling the chill seeping into my clothes. Goose bumps started to form on my arms and I shivered. Was that only the cold? I took a breath of chilled air and let it out again, but the odd feeling that had come over me wouldn't go away. It felt like someone was watching me, and that's not normally a sensation a witch ignores. I abruptly decided that I had enough photographs and I had to get out of there, but with all the shelves and tables everywhere, I must've gotten turned around. The warehouse felt like a maze. I started walking down a corridor, telling myself, *don't freak out, don't freak out, don't freak out* when I turned the corner and . . .

Okay, here comes a freak-out.

A man was handcuffed to a metal chair in his underwear,

with frozen blood on the floor around him. A trail of foot-prints led off behind him.

I knew his face; I'd been looking at it ten minutes ago. He was Holt Everand, one of the Butter Festival competitors. The blue eyes that had sparkled on the flyer were wide open and lifeless. His mouth hung open, making him look like he was surprised about something. On the table next to him was a clawed hammer, the end matted in blood and pieces of blond hair.

He was dead. Most definitely, absolutely, no-doubt-about-it dead.

I heard a noise behind me. I had my camera in my hands and in shock pressed the button, taking a photograph of Holt. The flash burst out, leaving me blinking away stars in my vision.

I whirled around but I couldn't see anyone.

Holy crap, was the murderer still in the building?

The glare of the flash faded enough for me to peer at my phone. There was no signal—probably the warehouse, but possibly also the magical energy that swirled around Harlot Bay. It didn't play well with telecommunications.

I stood still, listening for any sound, but all I could hear was my heart thudding. I was clenching my camera like a weapon. After thirty seconds of standing there in the cold, I decided I really needed to get out of there to call the police.

I quickly glanced behind me at Holt. He was still in his chair, still dead, still surrounded by frozen blood on the floor. I looked down and found I was standing on blood droplets.

Okay, murder blood on my shoes, I'm done!

I bolted back the way I came, convinced someone was going to jump out at me at any moment and I'd throw a fire-ball at them in a panic. It got worse the closer I got to the exit —now is the point where I'd be bashed by a hammer. I ran the final feet to the door, shoved it open and burst out into the warm morning.

I quickly dialed the Harlot Bay sheriff's office and got put through to Sheriff Hardy. I told him I'd found a dead body, and he told me to stay where I was. It only took a few minutes for the police cars to arrive, and in that time the smudge of frozen blood on the side of my shoe had warmed up enough to trickle down onto the ground.

Gross.

Sheriff Hardy got out of his car and walked over. He looked down at the blood smeared on my shoe and then back up my face.

He's a solid man in his early fifties, and I've known him since forever, but that didn't stop me from shrinking under his patented police chief gaze.

"Someone killed Holt Everand. He's one of the Butter Festival competitors," I said.

"Stay right where you are, Harlow," Sheriff Hardy told me.

He instructed his men to cover all of the exits of the building and then they went inside. I stayed *literally* where I was. Some more of the frozen blood on my shoes melted down onto the ground before Sheriff Hardy returned and went back to his car. He came back with a couple of giant plastic evidence bags.

"Going to need you to step out of your shoes and put these on."

He was holding a pair of blue cotton shoe coveralls, the type that you might see a doctor in a hospital wearing. Something so I didn't contaminate the crime scene more than I already had.

Once I was out of my shoes (I guess they were evidence now) and wearing bright blue cotton, Sheriff Hardy led me to his car.

"So, Harlow, can you tell me how it is you came to be in a warehouse with a dead body?"

I told Sheriff Hardy about coming to the warehouse to get photographs of the butter and how upon finding the front door locked, I'd gone around to the side.

"It didn't occur to you that if the front door was locked that perhaps you should wait until someone arrived to unlock it?"

"I wasn't intending to break in. I just happened to walk down the side. There was an open door. Besides, it's a warehouse. I thought that someone would be there. I took some photos of the butter."

"I'll need a copy of your photographs. Can you bring them to the station? You didn't see anyone? Hear anyone?"

"I heard a noise, waited a bit to see if I heard it again, and then got out of there."

Sheriff Hardy blew out air between his lips and then rubbed his hands through his hair.

"Well, the man in there is definitely dead. We probably won't be able to say exactly when he died because he's nearly frozen. How did you know his name?"

I pulled the Butter Festival flyer out of my pocket and gave it Sheriff Hardy. He read through some of the bios of the competitors, his eyebrows inching up higher.

"Zero Bend, huh? Well, that explains the crime we just discovered."

"What crime?"

"Someone went on a graffiti spree last night. You didn't see it?"

Graffiti spree? John had mentioned it to me, but I hadn't noticed anything out of the ordinary on my walk through town. On the other hand, I'd almost stomped on a group of six-year-olds, so it was entirely possible I wasn't paying attention very well.

"Must have missed it," I said.

"Take a walk down the main street later."

He gave back the Butter Festival flyer and made some notes about what I'd told him.

"I'll get a statement typed up for you to sign. Let me know if you remember anything else that could be useful."

"Oh, okay," I mumbled, feeling a distant part of me wonder if this was what shock felt like.

I needed my cousins. I needed proper shoes. I needed to get away from the liquid drops of red blood that I'd tracked onto the ground.

I nodded to Sheriff Hardy and walked away. When I turned the corner, I saw the graffiti John and the sheriff had mentioned. It was difficult to explain how I'd missed it.

Fluorescent orange letters were painted at least a foot high on multiple shop windows, the same name over and over again.

ZERO BEND

CHAPTER SIX

"What are you wearing on your feet?" Molly asked me.

I sat down on the sofa and took a deep breath. The day was warm, but the cold air of the freezer seemed clogged in my lungs.

"I saw a dead body," I began, peeling the booties off.

I told Molly and Luce about finding Holt Everand dead and practically frozen in the warehouse and hearing someone before I got out of there.

"Then Sheriff Hardy took my shoes because they had blood on them."

Molly had her hands up covering her mouth. Luce was clenching an empty cup with white knuckles.

"Do you think the killer saw you?" Luce asked.

"I heard a noise . . . maybe someone saw me."

The thought was chilling. What if—

"What if they saw you and followed you back here so they could get rid of any witnesses!" Luce yelled.

"Calm down," Molly snapped at her.

"Calm down? *Calm* down? There could be a psycho ice warehouse killer out there watching us right now!"

Luce dramatically pointed out the front window.

Across the street, old Mrs. Osterman was shuffling along behind her equally elderly terrier, Rumtum. He was wearing a plaid jacket that protected him from the weather. A light puff of wind would have taken both of them down.

"Pretty sure it wasn't Mrs. Osterman," I said.

"Yeah? That's how they get you. It's always the person you least suspect."

"Well, in that case, we should tell Sheriff Hardy to round up all the six-year-olds in town, because I saw a bunch of them this morning, and they were cute and adorable and definitely not on my murder suspect list."

"This was a methodical killing," Luce murmured to herself.

I decided to ignore her until she came back to reality.

"What did Sheriff Hardy say about it?" Molly asked.

"Not much. They're investigating. From the frozen blood, he could have been killed any time in the past day."

". . . probably lunatics traveling cross-country, bashing in heads as they go . . . "

I gave her the Butter Festival flyer. Her eyebrows rose when she read Zero Bend's name.

"Did you see the graffiti?" she asked me.

"On my walk here. Pretty weird for him to graffiti his own name, though, right?"

". . . network of serial killers, filming their kills, sharing them online . . . "

"He does look weird. Wasn't he the guy who threw someone out a third-story window?"

"Haven't done my research yet. The photos were my first work."

". . . draining the blood of the living, making some creepy spell most likely . . . "

The photos! I'd completely forgotten about them despite Sheriff Hardy asking me to bring a copy to the station.

I opened my bag and pulled out my camera. It looked big and expensive, but actually it was about third-hand, slower than a wet week sometimes, and I really wanted to upgrade it. I flipped out the small view screen.

"I took a whole lot of photos before I found the body! Maybe there's something in them."

Molly came over to sit beside me as I scrolled through the images.

". . . need to close the town borders, trap the murderer here, hunt them down . . . "

"Butter, more butter, butter from a different angle," I muttered. The view screen wasn't very big, only a few inches across, so I'd have to double-check them later, but I was fairly sure I hadn't accidentally caught a murderer in the background leering at me from the shadows.

Luce finally stopped talking to herself and sat down on my other side to look through the images.

"You took a lot of butter photos," she said as I zoomed through another twenty or so.

"I don't think there's anything here—"

I hit the final photo. The one I took accidentally when I pressed the button in shock.

It showed the warehouse, the frozen pool of blood, the neat butter packages, and . . . no Holt Everand.

Just a black aura, like a hole in reality, where he should have been.

CHAPTER SEVEN

*M*olly's spare shoes were pinching my toes, and I tried not to pace the park while I waited for the Butter Festival's grand opening.

After seeing the black hole where Holt should have been, there was perhaps a mini-freakout at Traveler involving three witches. Then we calmed down and I copied all the images to a memory stick for the sheriff—except for the last one. Molly lent me her sneakers and I left to go to Scarness Park for the grand opening.

Scarness Park is down on the foreshore and not surprisingly right next to Scarness Beach. There was a permanent stage built near a children's playground, and adjoining that were a few free public-use barbecues.

Behind the stage are rocks that form the break wall and then the beach and calm water. The tide was going out. In the distance you could see Truer Island. A few lazy seagulls drifted on the virtually nonexistent breeze. A fat pelican floated on the rapidly disappearing water.

It was a beautiful day and a wonderful time to be alive . . . for anyone who hadn't seen a dead body recently.

I was calm . . . sorta. The idea that someone bad had seen me at the warehouse wasn't sitting very well in my stomach.

Behind the crowd was a huge object hidden by a black sheet. It was protected by a guard rope and assistants dressed in all black. Presumably it was the giant chunk of ice that Zero Bend would carve.

I turned back to the stage and looked up at the banner proclaiming "Butter Festival" in bright red and blue letters. All around me were tourists, locals who supported the festival, locals with nothing better to do, and locals who disapproved of it (Hattie Stern). She'd pursed her lips at me when I caught her eye. There were also a bunch of girls dressed in punk clothing that was very short and revealing.

Without warning, throbbing bass burst out of the speakers. BOOM-cha-BOOM!

The mayor leapt up on the stage and received a hero's welcome. He took the microphone.

"Buuuuuuuuuuuuuuutttttttttttttteeeeeeeeeeerrrrrrr!" he called out like he was inviting a wresting superstar to the stage.

The crowd cheered again. I found myself getting caught up in it. Yeah, butter carving! It's amazing!

"The man of the hour to open the festival, Preston Jacobs!"

The mayor whipped the crowd up into a frenzy—well, most of the crowd. Hattie Stern was still sucking lemons.

Preston Jacobs bounded up onto the stage.

We're a seaside town, so tans aren't that unusual here, especially with our magically influenced weather, but Preston Jacobs had taken it to a whole new level. He was *glowing*, his skin somewhere between leather brown and bright orange. His hair was yellow. Not blond. Not white. It was like the sun had burst on his head. He took the microphone, shook the mayor's hand and smiled at the crowd. All I saw was gleaming white teeth before I had to close my eyes, afterimages floating behind my eyelids. I blinked away the glow coming from his perfect mouth and saw his eyes, a vivid sparkling blue so vibrant there was no way it could be real.

"Thank you, Harlot Bay!" Preston called out, his voice echoing across the crowd. He had a slight accent, a twang from somewhere further south that suggested that while he looked like a surfer, perhaps he might rope cattle too and had a *yeehaw* cocked and ready to go.

He moved behind the podium and put the microphone in its holder. The thick gold watch on his wrist gleamed.

"Welcome to the Harlot Bay Butter Festival. This week we're going to be seeing some of the world's greatest artists fighting it out to win this"—he gestured to a giant trophy sitting at the back of the stage—"and also take home five hundred thousand dollars!"

The crowd went crazy, and he raised his arms like a tele-vangelist at the front of a congregation.

Preston leaned down over the podium, smiling warmly, the skin of his face so tight it looked like it might snap at any moment. He was unnaturally smooth. My guess: extensive plastic surgery.

"You know, folks," he said, his voice dropping down, "I lived in Harlot Bay many years ago, and I can't think of a better place to hold this championship. This town, *this beach*, was where I played as a kid and where I got the idea to sell sandcastle-making supplies. In a way, Harlot Bay gave me everything, and so when Greco Romano"—a scattered cheer went up—"called me, I said yes immediately. Thank you, Harlot Bay, for your welcome, and in return we hope to provide you with art that challenges, art that amazes, art that changes your conception of what art truly is."

He finished off with his voice nearly at a whisper. Everyone leaned in.

"And now, to show us something incredible, we have a multitalented sculptor who has not only broken every boundary of our art form, but has taken it in new and amazing directions. I give you ice carving with the one, the only . . . Zero Bend!"

From behind us, heavy rock music burst out, and the entire crowd turned as one. The huge object under the black sheet was now surrounded by assistants. They pulled away the barriers and the sheet to reveal a gigantic block of ice standing on a steel platform. Industrial-strength coolers sat around it, blowing freezing air over it to stop it from melting.

As they pulled the sheet away, they revealed a man sitting in a silver chair.

Zero Bend.

He was young, maybe late twenties, if that, and his hair was a riot of spikes and vivid colors. His ears, nose, lips and chin were all pierced with gold and silver jewelry. He was wearing ripped jeans and multiple rings, and his fingernails were painted black. He had on giant black sunglasses that were studded in what looked like diamonds.

A girl wearing 1950s swing dancing clothes—a big skirt, a red checkered top, black-and-white shoes, white socks, a kerchief in her hair and red lipstick—appeared from the trailer parked behind the block carrying a chainsaw. She walked over to Zero and tried to pass it to him, but he didn't respond. He was slumped in his chair like he was either dead or asleep.

I felt a twist of cold in my stomach. *Please be asleep, please be asleep. Hungover. I'll take dead drunk hungover rather than . . . dead. I can't see two dead bodies on the same day.*

The girl slapped him in the face but he didn't move. His head lolled.

Oh no.

She started the chainsaw and held it up above her head, revving it. The crowd murmured in excitement. The chainsaw was loud, but so was my heart, thudding like crazy.

The girl brought the running chainsaw down on Zero Bend in a savage swipe that seemed sure to cut him in half. The crowd screamed and suddenly Zero was up, twisting the girl and chainsaw in one smooth move. She stumbled away from him and then turned it into a cartwheel and he raised the chainsaw up with one hand and grinned at the crowd.

His teeth were gleaming in pure gold.

Zero ran at the block of ice and swung the chainsaw. It connected with a crunch and a spray of ice that covered the crowd. As we watched, he hacked like a madman, making seemingly random cuts, ice shards flying everywhere. He was dressed in black but soon was covered in what looked like snow.

There seemed to be no pattern to his cutting. He'd shove the chainsaw in deep, rev it up, scrape it down a side, twirl it from one hand to the other, throw it in the air and catch it . . . and suddenly it was over.

The chainsaw went dead and Zero was left standing where his chair was, his head down, panting, covered in ice chips. The ice block looked pretty much the way it was before. It was still square, but now it glimmered with a pattern of internal cuts.

The swing girl walked up to Zero and then looked at the crowd. She put her hands up like, "What is this supposed to be?"

Zero suddenly moved, hurling the chainsaw at the block and grabbing the girl at the same time. He dipped her deep and kissed her.

The chainsaw hit the block and it shattered, chunks of ice falling to the ground leaving behind . . .

Zero Bend and Swing Girl carved in ice, locked in a passionate embrace.

I couldn't help gasping along with the crowd. It was perfect. Every line of her dress, her legs, her soft lips. His spiky hair, his clothes, even the laces on his thick boots. It was dynamic, like the ice couple were about to break out of their kiss and run away at any moment.

The real Zero pulled the girl up and stood there for a moment with her, their foreheads touching.

Then the assistants rushed in with big black sheets to cover Zero and Swing Girl as they ran for their waiting car.

We were left with their ice duplicate, a kiss frozen in a perfect moment.

I looked around the crowd, seeing the wonder on everyone's faces, and then a scruffy shape resolved itself into Jack Bishop. He had glints of ice in his hair. Our eyes met in the perfect moment of silence before the crowd went crazy and started cheering.

CHAPTER EIGHT

I left Scarness Park telling myself I did not, *did not* need to be spending time talking with a tourist. I arrived at the Harlot Bay police station to find Carter Wilkins sitting in the waiting area. His already-sour face creased up when I walked in and his eyebrows started that twitchy Morse code thing again. I decided to annoy him.

"Hi, Mr. Wilkins! How are you today?" I said, beaming at him like he was my long-lost best friend.

I saw the internal battle cross his face. He actually was a decent reporter, and therefore he surely knew I'd been the one to discover the body. His archrival was also the main primary source. How delicious.

"Good afternoon, Harlow," he finally ground out.

The receptionist, Mary, nodded at me as I took a seat.

"What's new?" I asked Carter.

He bit his lip and then blew air out between his lips before summoning up . . . was that his attempt at a smile? He ended up looking like a nervous dog.

"I could ask you the same thing. I understand you found the body of Holt Everand this morning?"

I let him hang for a moment. He only held his fake smile for a few more seconds before being forced to let it go.

"I did."

"Could you tell me what time that was? What did you find?"

He flipped open a notebook and clicked his pen.

"Oh, in the morning I found Holt Everand dead. You'll be able to read all about it online shortly."

I don't know what message his eyebrows were sending out, but I bet it had a lot of cursing in it.

I saw him try to push out another smile, but clearly those rarely used muscles had exhausted themselves. He settled for flat with a slight frown.

"I'd love to interview you for my paper," he said. "Care to give a comment?"

I'm not malicious, not really, but sometimes perfect moments arrive, and if you don't take advantage of them, how can you look at yourself in the mirror in the morning? This was one of those perfect moments. I could almost hear Aunt Cass's sarcastic voice in my mind.

"Well, I think—"

My perfect moment was obliterated by a tall blond man wearing an immaculate black suit sweeping into the police station and demanding to see Sheriff Hardy immediately.

"What is it regarding?" Mary asked.

"My client, Zero Bend, and Mr. Holt Everand!"

I noticed he had a single fingernail painted red on his right hand. The middle one.

Carter leapt out of his chair like a sprinter off the blocks. He practically teleported to the man's side.

"You're Zero Bend's agent? Do you have any comment on the graffiti featuring his name through our town?"

I fumbled my recorder out of my bag and joined Carter. I

was still stinging a little at missing my perfect comeback, but my reporter instincts were kicking in.

Before the man could answer, Sheriff Hardy appeared with a folder in his hand.

"Carter, Harlow, this is Mr. Swan," Sheriff Hardy said.

"Fusion Swan, artist agent," he corrected, holding out his hand to me. "And you two are Harlot Bay's media! Print and digital working side by side, I love it."

I shook his hand. It was cold and dry.

"We don't work together," Carter said sourly.

I'm pretty sure he would have despised me simply for competing with him, but there was also history there. When I'd returned to Harlot Bay, I'd gone for a job interview at his one-man paper. The interview was going fine until I asked if he was planning to move to an online edition at all. You would have thought I'd handed him one of Hattie Stern's lemons to suck on the way his face contorted. The interview went downhill quickly after that, and I decided I didn't want to work there as much as he didn't want me either.

Then I started up the *Harlot Bay Reader* and from some of the comments Carter has thrown my way, he apparently believes my job interview was actually a spying mission. I extracted valuable business intelligence, and essentially any good ideas behind my online newspaper were stolen from him. Or something like that. When we do cross paths, he hardly speaks to me, as though I'm going to steal every golden sentence right out of his mouth. I'm very fine with this arrangement and wish he'd go the whole way to the complete silence package.

"Competition! Excellent idea. Sharpen your weapons against each other. The struggle for dominance makes us all better. I love it."

He turned to Sheriff Hardy. "I need to speak with you urgently."

"Yes, your multiple phone messages told me that."

Sheriff Hardy looked over the three of us before letting out a sigh.

"Okay, we'll all go down here. Get this done in one go. Follow me."

We went down to a medium-sized conference room. The Harlot Bay police department isn't very big, despite some of the weird crimes that go on here, so the room felt very unused. There was dust on the table in the middle of the room.

Once we all sat down, with Fusion, me and Carter on one side of the table, Sheriff Hardy cleared his throat and began.

"Holt Everand was found dead this morning by a local news reporter taking photos for the Butter Festival. We are treating the case as a homicide. Mr. Holt suffered a head wound from a single strike to the back of his skull and appears to have died due to blood loss. We believe the crime took place last night, but due to the chilled environment, we cannot pinpoint a time. Workers delivering butter were last in the warehouse a day earlier, so that is our timeline. We currently have no suspects, but we are actively pursuing leads. That's all I can tell you."

He pointed a finger at Fusion.

"Go."

"Mr. Everand was a client of my agency, and we're willing to provide any help we can to solve this. You are aware a number of people were feuding with him, correct?"

"We are. We'd like a list from you, if possible. Anyone you think might have a motive here."

"Motive? How about five hundred thousand dollars in prize money? The prestige and sponsorships that will come from winning the butter-carving championship? Want a list of suspects? Here they are."

He slipped the Butter Festival flyer out of his pocket and slid it across the table to Sheriff Hardy.

"You represent Mr. Bend also? We'd like him to come down for an interview."

Fusion leaned back and shrugged. "He's an artist—very temperamental. I will ask him, but he traditionally doesn't get along well with law enforcement."

"Did Zero Bend graffiti his name everywhere for publicity?" Carter blurted out.

"We don't know who did that. He is incredibly popular. I suspect someone who loves his bad boy style got a little excited. There are a group of fans who follow him around the world, you know. They call themselves the Ice Queens, but they are definitely not cold, if you get my drift."

Fusion said that last bit to me and even winked. Yuck. With every word out of his mouth he was transitioning from a real person to a fake one. It was like watching a bad play.

Now the very underdressed girls at the Butter Festival's opening made sense.

"Mr. Swan, the *Harlot Bay Times* would like an exclusive interview with you," Carter said.

"Exclusive? I'll tell you what: I'll send both of you fine journalists a press release and see how you report on it tomorrow. Whoever does the best job will receive the exclusive interview. Fair?"

I mumbled something that could have possibly been *yes*. My reporter side was telling me to get that interview for the story. My witch side was bugs-crawling-on-my-skin itchy and didn't want to spend any more time with this guy at all.

Carter turned to Sheriff Hardy.

"Do you have any clues as to the identity of the vandal?"

"We're looking into it. Due to the popularity of the festival, we have a lot of tourists in town, and we are aware this has occurred at other locations Mr. Bend has traveled. As

Mr. Swan said, there may be some excited fans out there. We're going to find the culprit and *anyone who directed their actions* and pursue them with the full force of the law. Let's just hope no one is stupid enough to do it again."

The way Sheriff Hardy said it, I knew he didn't believe for one second that it was some random groupie or crazy fan. And that last bit? A clear warning to Fusion Swan.

Sheriff Hardy pointed at me.

"Harlow?"

Oh, what questions did I have? Um . . . none, really. I'd found the body, and so I had known most of what he'd said already. I reached into my bag and pulled out the memory stick with the photos on it. I slid it across the table.

"Here are the photos I took this morning before I found Mr. Everand," I said.

"I want a copy of those!" Carter said quickly.

"These are crime scene photos and I'll decide if we release them, if at all."

"It's not fair! She's going to report on this murder, and she has the crime scene photos and I don't?"

I turned to Carter, my mouth hanging open in disbelief.

"Are you kidding? I was *there*, that's why I have the photos. And I'll tell you this: there's nothing in them. It's all just butter, piles and piles of butter."

I left out my final photo of the gaping black hole in reality where Holt Everand had been.

"It's bias and I won't stand for it," Carter sniped.

Sheriff Hardy sighed and rubbed his face. Last year Carter had written an article that strongly hinted at some sort of corruption "high up" in the Harlot Bay police force. The evidence to base this vague attack on? An "unnamed source" within the department had advised that local businesses provided generous benefits to the police. Big Pie Bakery was named as one of these businesses, and when my mother and aunts marched down to Carter's office, he accused them of giving the police seven donuts when they only ordered six.

Yup, corruption from up on high.

I'll say this for Carter: he has some guts to face down three angry witches.

The craziest thing that happened after that was while the aforementioned three angry witches were cooking up a revenge plot, Aunt Cass told them to stop being babies and said that any publicity was good publicity. She pretty much banned them from fighting back, and she was probably right. Sales at the bakery increased after that.

"I will look at the photographs, and if they do not contain anything we wish to keep to ourselves for the moment, I will have Mary send you a copy. I suspect you will have to ask Harlow's permission to publish them, however, as she is the one who owns the copyright."

"I do not give my permission to publish," I said to Carter sweetly.

"Bias," he muttered to himself.

Sheriff Hardy stood up. The meeting was over.

"Unless there is anything else, I need to get back to work. Mr. Swan, if you could arrange with your client to come down here, I would appreciate it. Harlow, may I talk with you a moment about a different matter?"

"Looking forward to those articles," Fusion said, pointing at me and Carter before leaving.

Carter stopped in the doorway. "I'm not going to put up with bias," he declared before marching away, his eyebrows twitching like crazy.

Sheriff Hardy waited until they were gone before sitting down again. He reached over and turned off my recorder.

"This is not for print. Holt was drained of blood, and I

mean almost completely. He had some other kind of liquid in his veins, which we've yet to identify."

"He was sitting in a frozen puddle of blood."

"A little bit of blood goes a long way. The rest of it was gone. Take a look at this."

Sheriff Hardy opened the folder he'd brought in and slid a photo across to me. It was the back of Holt Everand's neck, the photo taken on the autopsy room table. He had a huge bruise in the shape of a handprint across his neck. You could clearly see the finger marks.

"What do you make of that?"

I examined the photo for a moment but didn't get more out of it than I'd already seen.

"That's a bruise in the shape of a hand."

"A bruise is blood that has been drawn to the surface of the skin. Do you know . . . anything . . . that might cause such an injury?"

Sheriff Hardy looked at me, and I suddenly understood he was talking about witch-related matters. There are rumors aplenty about our family, and the way our decrepit mansion looms over the town certainly doesn't help, nor do the various shenanigans/possible crimes Aunt Cass has pulled over the years. Sheriff Hardy's family has lived in Harlot Bay as long as ours has, and he knows all the stories. He also knows that sometimes our family can help when traditional methods of investigation have failed. I'm not sure of all the details, but I know Aunt Cass has helped him out in exchange for him over-looking certain events the police might otherwise be interested in (such as her illegal fireworks business she was running for a while and sometimes starts up again when she feels like it).

It's one of those "he knows, we know, *he* knows *we* know, *we* know *he* knows" situations. He'll never come right out and say it, so this is where we end up: an online journalist being asked questions outside her official circle of knowledge.

"I . . . may be able to find out something about that. I'll check with some of my sources," I told him.

He nodded and slipped the photo back into the folder.

"Thanks, Harlow. Hey, I hear the sisters are possibly renovating the mansion to start a bed-and-breakfast?"

How did he know that? I'd only heard about it last night.

"Um . . . yeah. My mom seems pretty excited about it. They baked a cake in the shape of the house to break the news."

"Well, it sounds great. We definitely need good business development in this town."

I felt a whoosh as my stomach dropped. I'd heard Ro make that exact statement just last night. Not sorta-that-statement. The *exact* statement.

"Have you been talking with my aunts about this?" I asked.

"Down at the bakery; I go in there a lot. We get to talking," Sheriff Hardy said a little too quickly.

I regarded him with my patented I-know-you're-lying-to-me face, but Sheriff Hardy is a pro. He wasn't going to crack anytime soon.

Our three fathers had all left our mothers within the same year, and Molly, Luce and I make it a point *not* to know anything about the moms' respective love lives if we can help it. All three of them have only two settings: sneaking around or too-much-information. An innocent question about a strange car parked outside the house might lead to a conversation you really didn't want to be in.

Aunt Ro and Sheriff Hardy?

I've known him forever. He is a good man through and through, but in my mind he was always the friendly police officer. I'd never imagined him out on a date, and fitting Aunt Ro into that scenario seemed very strange.

Imagine if they got married! We had a hard enough time keeping our witchiness suppressed and under the radar. I wonder how *that* conversation between them would go.

"They do make good baked goods," I said finally. This wasn't over, and I just couldn't wait to tell Molly and Luce. Turning the romantic meddling powers of my mom and Aunt Freya on Ro might get them off our collective backs.

Sheriff Hardy stood up and cleared his throat. Standing up was a really effective way to end a meeting. I needed to remember that.

"Well, thanks for coming in and supplying the photographs. Let me know if your sources have any information they'd like to share."

"I'll do that," I said and *winked for some reason* and then nearly combusted in embarrassment before scurrying out of there.

CHAPTER NINE

J rushed back to my office. John was elsewhere, which was good because I needed to concentrate on writing my article about Holt Everand. I had the jump on Carter Wilkins by a day *and* I was a primary source too. I needed to take advantage of this.

I found an email waiting for me from the Swan Agency. It contained two press releases, one on the untimely death of Holt Everand and the other about Zero Bend, a volatile artist who had nothing to do with the recent graffiti in Harlot Bay.

Both of the press releases were pure advertising and I decided to use none of it. Fusion Swan and his agency were clearly experts at media manipulation.

With that in mind, I headed out into ye olde Internet for some research. I admit, being a reporter isn't as cool as it used to be. Secret meetings in underground parking garages, midnight rendezvous, and frantic car chases had all been replaced with the reporter sitting in front of a computer, tapping away at a keyboard. You see it all the time in movies. They add a fast-paced thudding song behind it, but there is just no way to make searching on the Internet as thrilling as a secret meeting in an old barn.

Firstly, Zero Bend. Alongside clips of him butter carving, ice carving, and stone sculpting were a thousand gossip sites following his every move. *Zero Bend breaks up with Saskia!* No last name, just Saskia. She looked vaguely familiar. *Zero Bend in Drunken Brawl! Zero Bend Throws Girlfriend Out Third-Story Window!*

I read through that one. A few months back, at the Russian Sand Carver International, Zero had allegedly thrown his girlfriend (another model, one-word name: Issa) out the window. They were staying on the third floor. She landed in the swimming pool and refused to press charges.

I kept reading Zero Bend stories, and they all shared a common theme: violence and aggression. He was constantly fighting with paparazzi, starting bar brawls, smashing expensive vases, or being found drunk and asleep in a child's treehouse. In all the articles he was called a genius, brilliant, and amazing . . . but also drunk, violent, and obsessed. He'd once beaten up a carving festival organizer for not chilling the butter correctly.

The Bad Boy of Sculpting indeed.

His rivalry with Holt Everand popped up here and there. The thing with a guy like Zero was that he had about a thousand feuds going at any time. Apparently, he and Holt had come to blows in Tokyo after Zero carved a statue of Holt's girlfriend—her face on the body of a pig. Holt had punched Zero in the face and they'd both been disqualified.

So . . . Holt and Zero come to Harlot Bay to compete, and Zero goes to the butter storage warehouse to check that everything is up to his high standards. He finds Holt is already there, an argument breaks out, he clobbers Holt with a hammer . . .

It was plausible. Both he and Holt were known to be

perfectionists, so it was reasonable that they'd visit the warehouse to confirm everything would be correct. The tying-to-the-chair bit, though? The blood-bruise handprint and the missing blood—not so clear if Zero Bend did that.

I spent the next hour diving into the world of butter carving, stone sculpting and associated art forms (sand sculpting, jelly slicing, ice carving). It was definitely one of those things you have no idea is so big until you get into it. The prize money for some of these competitions was a million dollars. The sculptors would compete for money and prestige, and the winners were often commissioned to create art for major companies and rich people. A Wall Street investment firm had paid Zero $800,000 for a sculpture titled *Dark Coin*.

Zero Bend was a rich, genius, violent, drunken artist—but was he a murderer?

It was a question for another day. I had work to do, and if I wasn't careful I'd spend a thousand years online. I printed off the photo of the black hole where Holt Everand should have been and stuffed it in my bag. I wrote a puff piece about the Butter Festival opening, which included my photos of Zero Bend's incredible ice carving, and published it. Then I wrote a quick headline—*Holt Everand, Butter Festival Competitor, Found Dead in Harlot Bay Warehouse*—and typed like the wind, whipping up an article. It took me maybe half an hour of writing, and then I spent another half hour checking my work. It's the story of a one-woman online newspaper: I'm a journalist, photographer, editor, publisher, salesperson, and every other job too.

It wasn't perfect, but what writing is? You do your best and move on.

I published it to the front page of the *Harlot Bay Reader* and called it a day.

CHAPTER TEN

*A*s my creaking car hauled itself up the driveway, I saw a truck with TRUER LANDSCAPING emblazoned down the side parked outside the house. Hmm. *Okay, don't leap to conclusions.*

I drove past Aunt Freya and my mom talking to a young, well-built guy with a mop of shaggy blond hair. They both looked at me. Our eyes met and I *knew* instantly that he was William, the landscaper Luce had been casually observing down at the gardens.

The mothers were meddling. Maybe, *maybe* they really did need some landscaping done, but even if that were true, they could have chosen anyone in town. This couldn't end well. I drove down to our end of the mansion and debated walking back to scout out what was happening. Then Adams appeared in the window, meowed at me and vanished.

Ah, the hiding game.

I opened the door and made a big deal of arriving home. Lots of stomping and loud noises. Sitting near my bedroom door was a laundry basket. Adams was hiding in it, crouched down with his pouncing face on.

"Adams? Are you here? I wonder where he is?" I said aloud, walking around.

I saw him huddle down, a look of glee on his furry face.

"I just can't see him anywhere. It's such a puzzle. He's normally here."

I walked closer to the basket, my hands on my hips, the essence of puzzlement. Adams twitched his ears.

He leapt out and grabbed my leg.

"Aha!"

"Argh!"

We roughhoused for a moment, me messing up his fur before I hauled him up and gave him a hug.

"I was hiding in the basket! You didn't see me!"

"You came out of nowhere!"

"Like a ninja! Hiya!"

I carried him purring into the kitchen to get a drink of water. Sitting on the counter was a brochure from an online coffee machine business.

The mothers again, meddling.

I moved the brochure into the middle of the counter (hey, I need to have some fun too) and got myself a drink of water. It was cold and delicious and I felt myself relax as the chilled water hit my stomach.

Cold water and a purring cat. Ahh.

I sat down on the sofa, put Adams in my lap and decompressed. So much had happened today: finding Holt Everand dead, the opening of the Butter Festival, the police station with Carter Wilkins, and that creep, Fusion Swan. I looked down at Molly's very aged, paint-spotted shoes. I'd have to buy myself some new shoes, because I doubted mine were coming back anytime soon. Even if they were, did I want murder blood on my shoes?

I remembered my bank balance and decided eh, it was just blood. What's the big deal?

It wasn't long before Molly and Luce arrived home.

Luce's face was white like she'd seen a ghost and she was babbling.

"Him, that was. He was. Here? Why was he here? Those witches, what are. Witches up to?"

"Translation: Luce's boy toy drove past us on the way up here," Molly said.

"Freya and Mom were out front talking to him when I got home."

"What? Why didn't you go spy on them?" Luce demanded.

I pointed to the purring and very comfortable cat in my lap.

"Exhibit A," I said, stroking his ears.

"Oh, those meddling witches," Molly said. I suppressed a smile. She'd found the coffee machine brochure. A moment later she tossed it into the recycling container.

"You're not even going to read it? What if you get questions?"

"We already ordered one. It's being express-shipped, and it is not an amateur machine. We bought a commercial one."

"Can you two forget coffee for a moment? This is an emergency! They invited William up here to snoop on him."

"Did he appear to be eating any kind of magic-potion-infused baked goods on the way down?" I asked.

Luce's eyes went wide.

"I don't think so. Did you see him eating anything? Oh no, they're going to make him eat a love donut, aren't they?"

"Love donut? Isn't that the name of a band?" Molly said, an evil grin on her face.

"If I go down, you're coming with me," Luce threatened.

Now it was time for Molly's face to turn pale.

"Calm down, no need to get crazy. They are renovating, so *maybe* they're getting landscaping done too. Even if they are snooping, we can keep it contained. We just need something to distract them. Is Aunt Cass up to anything?"

"Ooh, oh, pick me, pick me," I said, putting my hand up.

"Yes, the journalist with the indestructible cat."

"Okay, so I was talking with Sheriff Hardy today . . ."

I told them about his comment about *this town definitely needs good business development* and how Ro had said that at last night's dinner, but they didn't seem as convinced as I was that something was going on.

"I dunno . . . that's a stretch. He does go to the bakery all the time. For all we know, he picked it up from her and repeated it," Luce said.

"You weren't there. I caught him in a lie when I asked if he'd been talking to my aunts. He went all stone-faced cop a second later, but for a moment I saw the truth."

"The truth being . . . ?" Luce asked.

"The two of them are having a secret love affair!"

"Possibly," Molly said thoughtfully. "Mom has been going out to do yoga more on weeknights. Maybe she is sneaking in a quick visit to Sheriff Hardy."

"We should follow her tomorrow night," Luce said immediately.

"What if she catches us? She'll . . . I mean, she *probably* won't curse us, but she'll make us wish we'd been cursed because at least that ends at some point," Molly said.

"Aunt Ro? Please, when she's driving, her entire world becomes what is in front of the car. She won't catch us, and what will she do anyway? Either we catch her going to yoga or we catch her seeing Sheriff Hardy, in which case she'll beg us to keep it secret from nosy sisters one and two," I said.

"They make a special batch of donuts for him," Adams said from my lap.

"What do you mean a special batch?" Luce said.

"They put it aside for him every time he comes. It's just for him."

"Adams, think very carefully—did you ever see them putting anything magical into the donuts?" Luce asked.

Adams opened his eyes, and I recognized the sly look on his face. Here it comes—bribe time.

"I don't remember . . . perhaps some tuna would help my memory."

I swear this cat could have been one of those shifty informants in the past.

"Fine, I'll get tuna for you."

Luce went to the cupboard and opened a can, dumping it into a bowl. She put it on the counter. Adams jumped off my lap and up onto the counter, but he met Luce's blocking hand when he went to take a bite.

"First tell me if they put anything in the donuts."

"No," Adams said.

She frowned.

"What do you mean?"

"They don't put anything magical in his donuts. At least, I don't think so. How am I supposed to know? I'm just a cat. Can I eat my tuna now?"

I saw Luce flirt with the idea of reneging on her tuna deal, so I shook my head at her and raised my eyebrows. It was a sneaky move on Adams's part, but Luce was the one who'd made the bad deal. If she took the tuna away, I wouldn't hear the end of it until tuna was supplied.

"Fine, eat, you little cheater," she muttered and moved her hand. Adams happily complied.

I was filling Molly and Luce in on the extra information Sheriff Hardy had given me—missing blood replaced by some unknown fluid—when we suddenly heard a chattering of voices outside. The mothers pushed open the front door, moving at high speed. Aunt Cass came in after them and sat on the sofa.

"Harlow Torrent! You found a dead body and didn't call me!"

Mom squeezed me in a backbreaking hug, then Freya and Ro. I'd be lucky if I could walk in the morning.

"Your cousin found a dead body and you didn't tell us?" Freya said crossly to Luce and Molly, pointing her finger at them.

"It's her news, not ours," Molly said, shrugging.

The mothers turned back to me. It was like being under a heat lamp.

"I was just on assignment," I said weakly.

"Just on assignment, she says. Magic forbid you were spotted by a murderer who's coming to snuff you out. I'm putting up a protective enchantment," Mom said.

She lifted her arms in the air, but I leapt forward to stop her.

"No, it's okay. We don't need that. The murder happened hours before I got there. No protective enchantment, please."

Magic isn't like digging a hole and then it's done. It's more like digging the same hole every day, and you get tired the longer it goes on. Cast a protection spell today at 7 p.m. and tomorrow at 7 p.m. a wave of exhaustion will wash over you. And the next day at 7 p.m. And the next until you let it go. Witches have died trying to keep too many spells going for too long.

I saw Molly and Luce glance at me. They knew I didn't want to freak them out any more than they already were. I'd have to wait until I could get Aunt Cass alone to speak to her about the bruised neck, missing blood, and black hole aura problem.

Mom reluctantly put her arms down.

"You three stick together after dark," Ro said.

"No sneaking off to see boys," Freya added.

Molly opened her mouth to protest and then thought better of it. We didn't want to open *that* particular Pandora's box.

"They're fine. Together they can handle anything," Aunt Cass said from the sofa.

Six pairs of narrowing eyes focused on her. What was she up to?

"Well, they can. Don't make such a big deal about it. Bunch of wusses."

Wusses?

Mom turned back around to me, but evidently Aunt Cass's compliment-insult combo had knocked all the words out of her. She shook her head and recovered.

"Be safe. Don't get involved. Well, you're already involved, but don't go crazy with it."

One Torrent witch telling another Torrent witch not to go crazy with it? Sir Pot, I'd like you to meet Lord Kettle.

"How did you know *I* found the body?"

I swear I saw a flash of something on Aunt Ro's face. Guilt?

"It's all over town. Everyone knows," Aunt Ro said.

Hmm.

The mothers took off after that. Aunt Cass stopped in the door and pointed her finger at the three of us.

"Get involved. There's something hinky going on and you need to find out what it is."

Hinky?

She vanished into the night as fast as our mothers had.

"Did you see my mother? She was totally lying about where she heard the news. I think she *is* having an affair with Sheriff Hardy," Molly said.

"We definitely need to follow her tomorrow night. They

want to mess with our love lives, we mess with theirs," Luce said.

"What about my mom and Freya? Are they doing anything out of the ordinary?" I asked.

"Freya came back here a week ago in the middle of the day, and a man came to the house," Adams said through a mouthful of tuna.

We immediately leapt on him, but in typical cat fashion he didn't know anything else because he didn't care about the comings and goings of humans.

"What about Mom? Do you know anything about her?"

"She made me get out of the pizza oven," Adams said. He'd finished the tuna and moved across to the sofa for a complete bath.

I suddenly realized we'd let the thought of catching our mothers in various secret love affairs get the best of us. We had bigger fish to fry.

"I think Aunt Cass might know something about the murder. Or at least why Holt Everand didn't show up in my photo. She was acting odd. Well, *odder*."

"Yeah, that was weird," Molly said. "When was the last time she gave us a compliment?"

"She told me my hair didn't look as bad as it normally did," Luce said.

Aunt Cass's specialty: complinsults.

"She told me I was dressing well for 'someone of my size,'" Molly added.

I pointed at my hair. "I'm looking less mannish now that my hair is growing out."

"She told me I was a good fireworks guard—for a cat," Adams said, wiping a paw over his ear.

Fireworks? Great. Whenever one of her business ventures was shut down, discovered or otherwise squelched, she always fell back on illegal fireworks sales. I was ninety percent certain she was running a subnetwork of teenage fireworks dealers in the town.

"I'm going to ask her about the photo and the body when I can get her alone," I said.

"Maybe if you can get her interested in this, she'll forget that we apparently 'snitched' on her," Luce said.

"Yeah, good luck with that. I'm preparing anti-zit poultices and a balance potion and keeping my eyes open for anything strange happening to me," Molly said.

We decided to adjourn on the topic of the meddling mothers and our love lives and reconvene tomorrow to come up with a plan to follow Ro. On the subject of Holt Everand and Aunt Cass telling us to get involved, we weren't sure what else we could do right then. Finding out about the missing blood and the black aura had to wait until I could speak with Aunt Cass alone. What else did she expect us to do? Solve the crime ourselves?

I went to bed and Adams joined me, taking up his position at the end of the bed. He was still finishing his complete bath, licking the same spot on his shoulder he always licked multiple times before finally settling down.

I turned off the light and closed my eyes, a little apprehensive that I'd dream about being trapped in a cold warehouse with a dead body. But as I drifted off to sleep, I was transported back to Zero Bend's ice carving. A handsome, scruffy stranger was watching me as flakes of ice drifted down on the crowd like snowflakes.

CHAPTER ELEVEN

*A*fter a very quick breakfast alone—Luce and Molly were still sleeping—I got myself ready and rushed down to the main part of the mansion. The mothers would be at the bakery already, having left at some ridiculous time in the morning, so I'd be able to talk to Aunt Cass alone.

I found her in the lounge, sitting in her recliner reading a book titled *Starting Your Own Bed-and-Breakfast!* There was a big pile of books next to her on the same topic, and also others on renovations and architecture.

"Are these your books?"

"They were just sitting here. I'm reading them if that's okay. Or will I be *caught* reading now?"

She's a little crotchety in the mornings . . . afternoons . . . nights . . .

I picked up one of the books. It was from the Harlot Bay Library.

The mothers were definitely meddling in our love lives. First the landscaper and now this?

Yes, I could see how it appeared that I was taking a completely innocent and absolutely justified trip to the

82

library the wrong way, but I know my mom and her sisters. They were snooping on the librarian for sure.

But what to do about it? Tell Molly the mothers had her librarian in their sights? The resulting freak-out would only hamper her ability to help us spy on Ro tonight. I'd give it a day and then let her know. I put the book back and took the photo out of my bag.

"Can I get your advice on something?"

I handed the photo to Aunt Cass.

"That was supposed to be Holt Everand. He was tied to a chair in the warehouse."

Aunt Cass put her book down. She got up and started pacing the room.

"Looks like some sort of soul sucker got to him. Drained the energy right out. What else do you know?"

"Most of his blood was gone and replaced with some liquid they haven't identified yet. He had a bruise on the back of his neck in the shape of a hand."

"That's a soul sucker, alright."

She passed the photo back to me.

"So you don't know what it is?"

"I have a few ideas. It's like finding someone mauled to death. Was it a dog, a cat, a crazed monkey with a vendetta because it was forced to wear a little red coat and dance for tourists? We need more evidence before we can know what we're dealing with. Did it smell like cinnamon in the warehouse?"

A crazed monkey . . . ?

"Not that I remember."

"Did you notice an excessive amount of butterflies in the area?"

"I don't think I saw *any* butterflies."

"Hmm . . . did the air feel slippery at any point? Like it was wearing thin on a doorway to another plane of existence?"

"Slippery air? No, nothing like that."

Aunt Cass threw her arms up in the air. "Well, I'm out of ideas." She flopped down in her recliner and turned on the TV.

"But what am I supposed to do?"

"Don't get soul-sucked. Watch out for anyone trying to get you alone. Look for anyone who appears younger and fitter than they should be. Oh no, not this guy again."

She was frowning at a fictional police detective.

"We can't . . . use a finding spell or something? Is there any way to detect evil?"

Aunt Cass glanced sideways at me.

"Detect evil? A soul sucker isn't evil any more than a leech or a mosquito is. They're just doing what they were made to do."

"Someone *made* them?"

"Made, evolved, designed, planted by aliens—whatever you want to believe. Now shush, I'm watching this. Oh, and don't take a photo of me with that camera you have or you're in big trouble."

"I would never take a photo of you without permission," I lied.

"I know. Just like I'd never sell illegal fireworks."

I opened my mouth to say more, but Aunt Cass put up her finger in the universal *shush now* gesture. Fine, I'd shush. I left her there frowning at the police detective.

I drove to work, sorting through everything I knew about soul suckers. They don't *literally* suck your soul, more your life energy and/or blood until you die. Some are parasites that latch on and slowly consume their victims. Others are more like mosquitoes—they'll drink a bit of your energy and move on.

Ever feel completely normal and suddenly you go flat or your mood crashes? That's what a soul sucker feels like.

Okay, maybe you had a huge pasta lunch and it was a food coma. But sometimes—soul sucker.

I stopped briefly at work and saw that the Holt Everand story I had written yesterday was receiving a lot of visitors. More visitors equals more advertising dollars, which is a good thing. I squelched a tiny burst of guilt; someone was dead and I was indirectly profiting. If I could just report the news and be paid for that, I'd do it. But it's not the world we live in.

I locked up and walked to the center of town. This morning the Butter Festival competitors were competing in a two-hour semifinal in the town hall. Only the top eight of sixteen would go through. Then tomorrow they'd cut to four, then two, and then they'd compete in the Grand Finale. I was early, hoping I could get an interview with Zero Bend directly.

I paid my entry fee—no press privileges for an online newspaper—and went inside.

The Harlot Bay town hall is a multipurpose building; they sometimes play basketball there. It has stadium seating all around it, good lights, and a large, polished wood floor. There were sixteen areas set up for each of the competitors. They had one large table stacked high with butter and a flat carving surface. It was cold inside the hall and I wished I'd worn a jacket.

Each of the competitor areas was roped off, giving the hall the appearance of a maze. Some people were already wandering around looking at the butter piles. The stands were slowly filling with spectators.

I looked around the hall hoping to see Zero Bend, but I only saw Fusion Swan waving his arms at some young, scared male assistant dressed in all black. After the assistant scurried away, Fusion caught my eye and *whistled* at me to come over.

Great, called like a dog. Classy. I approached him, and when he held out his hand I shook it for some reason.

"Ms. Torrent, I read your article last night about Holt Everand and noticed you didn't use any of the material we sent you. Did you not want an exclusive interview?"

I glanced at his hand. Today the middle nail was painted blue. Urk.

"I'd like an interview with Zero Bend. Is he around?"

"He doesn't see anyone before a carve. He's meditating right now. Perhaps if we see a good article from you, we can arrange an interview, yes?"

The scared assistant returned with a glass of water. Fusion stared at it for a moment before sighing.

"Did I ask for ice?"

"Um . . . I . . . I thought—"

Fusion put up his hand.

"I asked for a glass of water. You brought me a glass of water with three ice cubes in it. What's next? Some chocolate sprinkles? Perhaps a stick of celery in it? Do as I ask, please."

He waved the assistant away and turned back to me.

"Big things are happening this week. A competitor murdered, his archrival in town, a significant amount of money up for grabs. I would think you'd do everything you could to snag an exclusive."

Was he implying his own client was a murderer?

I spotted Preston Jacobs over at the back of the hall talking with the mayor. I was *so* done with this slippery agent.

"Enjoy your stay in Harlot Bay," I rhymed to Fusion and walked away. Oops, still rhyming.

I didn't look back, even though I was sure I'd see him standing there confused that someone had declined his offer.

The mayor smiled at me as I approached him and Preston.

"Ah, Preston, you must meet Harlow Torrent. She runs the *Harlot Bay Reader*, the first and finest in online news for our region."

I shook Preston Jacobs's hand, and he smiled at me with those perfect white teeth.

Up close, he was practically humming with good health. His eyes were blue and twinkling, his skin was smooth, and he looked like he was ready to run ten miles without breaking a sweat. He even smelled good. He had to be in his late fifties or even early sixties, but he looked like a health and fitness guru.

"Torrent? You live up the hill, then?"

The mayor excused himself, ducking away in a flash. I glanced at the door and saw Hattie Stern standing there looking around. She never missed an opportunity to put forth her Harlot Bay name-change case to the mayor.

I nodded.

"Yes, we're those Torrents. The ones who run the Big Pie Bakery."

"The secret to enjoying simple carbs is to only eat carbs that are amazing. Big Pie is definitely in that group."

He grinned at me like we were in on the same secret.

"I'll tell my mom and aunts. They'll be very excited to hear that."

Preston smiled back at me again, and then his face turned solemn.

"I understand you were the one to find poor Holt in the warehouse. It's a tragedy. He was a champion sculptor. The world is less without him in it."

"Did you know him well?"

"Of course. I've been sponsoring various carving championships for years. I first met Holt at a lard carve in a tiny town in the middle of nowhere, if you can believe it. It was a million degrees, the cooling was failing, and this skinny kid turns in a perfect *Dreaming Iolanthe* version. He used his mother's face. It was spectacular. I knew right then and there he'd be a contender for the world championship."

I remembered *Dreaming Iolanthe* from my online research. Caroline Shawk Brooks had carved it in butter after reading a play and being inspired by the story's heroine. It had toured, yes *toured*, fairs where thousands of people paid twenty-five cents to see it. Eventually it ended up at the 1876 Centennial Exhibition in Philadelphia.

All this slipped through my mind in an instant. If I had a superpower, this would be it: I read really fast and remember a lot of what I read. Need facts about the Sunda Colugo (Malaysian flying lemur)? I did a project on them when I was *ten*.

"Do you know if anyone might have wanted him dead?"

At this, Preston frowned, his perfect forehead creasing as though the very idea of someone wanting to harm Holt was causing him physical distress.

"This isn't the first death we've had in the carving world, and it won't be the last. There is a lot on the line—reputation and money—and some people will do anything to win. *Cui bono?* I'd look at who benefits. Someone will from this, and perhaps they should be closely examined."

I had more questions, but the mayor reappeared and whisked Preston away to open the competition. I took a seat overlooking the hall and watched the one-two punch of the mayor and then Preston. They really were good. The two of them should tour.

Rock music played and the competitors emerged from the end of the hall. I recognized a few of them: Harmonious Twang, The Slice, Cold Rider. Zero Bend emerged last, carrying a silver metal suitcase. Across from me, an enormous roar came up from the crowd. It was the Ice Queens screaming and yelling like banshees. I saw with satisfaction that Hattie Stern was only sitting a few rows away from them. If they carved her face in butter it would be titled "Disapproval Extremis."

Right about then, just as Zero Bend was opening his suitcase to reveal many shiny knives and sculpting tools, I felt a prickle of magic. The hall was cold, but within a few seconds I was sweating.

Oh no, not now.

I took a few deep breaths of the chilled air, but I swear all it did was make me hotter.

This wasn't a spell someone was casting on me.

I was Slipping.

Slipping can be nothing—a tingle in the fingertips, a wash of goose bumps. Other times it's like the flu, all aching bones and running nose. When I was a kid, I'd tasted parsley for an entire day before suddenly being hit with nature witch power in a big way—I'd accidentally exploded a tree on our property by walking near it.

The lights in the hall flickered, and that was the final straw. I had to get out of there before something bad happened. I rushed down the stairs and through the hall, feeling like I'd just run a marathon in the desert. My face was already wet from sweating and my clothes were sticking to my skin. I glanced up at the crowd and saw Jack watching me with a puzzled frown. I ignored him and kept moving.

Soon I was out of the main hall and then I was outside. It was much warmer than inside, but it felt good.

That tiny bit of good feeling vanished as Hattie Stern appeared in front of me.

"Who did you touch?" she asked me.

I didn't have time for this. I tried to walk away, but she

grabbed my arm and then let go as though she'd been burned.

"Didn't Cassandra teach you anything? You're having an immune response right now."

I looked at her blankly, feeling my brain simmering inside my skull. Too hot, had to drink water. The fountain was nearby. I rushed over and splashed the cold water over my head.

Don't drink fountain water—basic knowledge drummed into us since we were kids. I turned off my overheated brain and gulped down the refreshing water.

By the time I was finished splashing myself with water and drinking, Hattie Stern was gone. I leaned against the fountain, feeling my temperature dropping. With each degree I felt my mind pulling back together.

That was an immune response? To what?

I'd only touched two people—Fusion Swan and Preston Jacobs. How could they possibly cause me to almost cook alive?

CHAPTER TWELVE

I decided I needed to talk with my cousins rather than return to my office alone. By the time I reached Traveler, my temperature was back to normal. My clothes were still damp from the fountain. I hoped I didn't get sick from drinking all that fountain water, but it couldn't be helped.

"We figured out your photo thing!" Luce announced as soon as I walked in. Molly thudded a heavy book down on the counter.

"*Kirlian Photography: Exploring Auras*," I read. "Is this some kind of mystical made-up pseudoscience thing?"

Molly flipped open the book to a picture of a kid surrounded by a gleaming blue aura.

"Dude, you're a *witch* in case you have forgotten. Mystical is your life. Look at this here!"

She flipped through a few pages showing pictures of children and adults surrounded by auras. The book explained what the colors and patterns meant.

"I don't know . . . ," I said dubiously.

Auras are real . . . we think. Growing up, I'd seen glimmers of color surrounding people—the joys of being a Slip witch—but it's not like we have a school that teaches you what it means. Aunt Cass says she sees auras, but she likes to brag about anything magical. If you told her you saw the moon, she'd say she walked on it. Always one-upping.

"Take a photo of me. See if you can get my aura," Molly said. She posed in front of the sofa, her hands on her hips.

I trained the camera on her and hit the button. A moment later the digital image appeared in the viewfinder. Molly was surrounded by a warm golden glow, like molten honey. There were tiny yellow sparks floating in it.

"This is amazing," Luce breathed. "Me next!"

She posed like a Japanese tourist on vacation—feet turned inward, big grin, peace sign.

Her aura was a rich purple streaked with lines of pale green.

I turned the camera on myself and took a picture.

"Wow, that's red," Molly said when the image appeared.

I was surrounded by a red aura as rough as a sea. The edge was curled up like waves, and there were floating red sparks that looked decidedly sharp.

"Okay, so I'm capturing auras now, until . . . whenever this goes away. What am I supposed to do with this?"

"Take a photo of Aunt Cass!" Molly said, rubbing her hands together deviously.

"Why?"

"Well, if it's sneaky looking, then we can use that to take her down a few notches."

"Define a sneaky aura."

"I don't know . . . one that looks suspicious. One that looks like it's hiding something."

I sighed and turned the camera off.

"Too bad she's already three steps ahead of us. When I

was talking with her this morning she told me not to take a photo of her."

"How does she know?" Molly mused.

"Ooh, you should take a photo of Jack-scruffy-and-handsome."

I opened my mouth to protest but then closed it again. It wasn't a bad idea.

"Why are you damp?" Molly asked, reaching out to touch my top.

"I was at the Butter Festival's first-round carve when I started to seriously overheat. Had to run outside and splash myself in the fountain to cool down."

"Ew, the fountain? Birds poop in there."

"That's just a myth your mother made up to stop us from drinking from it as kids."

"Why did you overheat?"

"Hattie Stern said it was an immune response. I thought I was Slipping."

I updated them on what Aunt Cass had told me about soul suckers. Then I told them about Hattie Stern and her "immune response" claim.

"So, what, Lemon Face is helping you now? That's weird," Molly said.

"I'd be more worried about the fever. You shook hands with the rich sandcastle guy and this sleazy agent, and no one else?"

"Just them, I'm sure."

"Could one of them be the murderer? Maybe a soul sucker?"

Luce glanced out the front window as though there'd be a hideous monster standing there watching us. I looked too. The street was empty. Not even an old lady and her dog this time.

If I had to pick one of the men to be a soul sucker, it

would be that sleazeball, Fusion Swan. He made my skin crawl just being near him. Very easy to dislike. On the other hand, Preston Jacobs was crazy fit and healthy for someone his age. Was being incredibly fit a sign of some dark entity? If it was, then there were some people down at the Harlot Bay Fitness Center who needed investigating.

"Maybe I should go back to the town hall and touch just one of them. See if it happens again."

"And if one of them is infested with some kind of spiritual leech?" Molly asked.

"Tell Sheriff Hardy, I guess. Maybe he could investigate, see if they were connected to the murder."

Even as I said it I could tell it was a long shot. I already had an answer for him as to missing blood, but I couldn't tell him it was probably some kind of magical entity. What would he even do with that information?

"Could be dangerous," Molly said, heading off to the back room.

I started flipping through the photography book while Luce neatened up the shop. Tourists like to touch everything but not buy much.

Aura photos: riding that thin line between pseudoscience and magic. Being that I was a Slip witch, this new power was likely to vanish at any random moment. If I wanted to use it, the clock was ticking.

I closed the book with an idea about following and photographing Preston and Fusion hovering on the edge of my mind, and I stared at nothing for a moment. That nothing became the Harlot Bay Library barcode on the back of the book.

"I see you've been to the library," I called out to Molly.

She appeared in the entrance to the back room, her hands full of fridge magnets.

"Thanks for helping us, Molly and Luce. Thanks for

figuring out my weird Slip power thing. Oh, that's okay Harlow, any time," she said.

"What is his name?"

"Whose name?"

"You know who."

"It's Oliver," Luce said from the sofa. "But she calls him Ollie."

"Nicknames? How cute. A spring wedding, then?"

Molly stuck her tongue out at me and returned to the back room.

I looked over at Luce, who was tapping away on her phone.

"Going to the gardens today?" I asked.

"Maybe. It's warm, so the outlook calls for shirts off."

"What are you going to do about the mothers calling up the landscaper?"

"We're going to ignore them."

"Since when has that worked?"

Luce shrugged.

Molly came in from the back room and dropped more magnets on the counter.

"It's a new strategy. I've been reading Sun Tzu's *The Art of War*, and then I read Carl von Clausewitz. 'Never engage the same enemy for too long or he will adapt to your tactics.' Our mothers keep snooping, we keep fighting them, and they learn our tactics. This time we're ignoring. They can prod and poke, but they won't get far because we won't give them anything."

I took a moment to digest this new bit of information.

"Why are you reading war strategy books?"

"She wants to appear smart to Ollie von Tight Pants," Luce said with a devious smirk.

"Let your plans be dark and impenetrable as night, and when you move, fall like a thunderbolt," Molly intoned.

"He is *so* into her. And there are a lot of girls at the library these days asking him for help."

"The supreme art of war is to subdue the enemy without fighting," Molly said and bowed to us both.

"So where does that leave us on following Ro tonight?"

"Oh no, that's still on. Intelligence gathering is essential," Molly said. She started sorting the magnets.

I pointed at Molly. "The man who carries a toaster will often ask you for bread."

"So useful," she said.

"A cat cannot be trusted to look after your fish."

"True."

I grabbed my bag and headed for the door.

"A beer in the hand is worth two in the fridge."

"Thank you, Harlow, nice to see you, goodbye now."

Molly came around the counter and shooed me outside. The door closed in my face.

"Do not drink and wax lest you lose more than you bargained for!" I called out, grinning.

CHAPTER THIRTEEN

J walked back to my office to swap the camera battery out. I didn't want it dying in the middle of photographing possibly bad people. When I got there, John was sitting on the sofa, *not* watching an infomercial for some kind of amazing stone-based cookware. He was normally entranced by the technological marvels of the home shopping network. As I watched, they threw plastic into a blazing hot frying pan and melted it down. A moment later they scraped it off with no problem. I swapped my camera battery and then looked at John. He was staring into nothing with a glazed look on his face.

"Hey, John, how are you?"

He looked at me as though he'd just woken up. "Good morning, Harlow. Why can't I die?"

Oh boy.

"What happened?"

"I threw myself in the grinder at Mahalo Seeds. It didn't do anything. So then I thought, why not get out of town? I hitched a ride in the back of some tourist's car, and just when we went outside the city limits, I suddenly found myself on the ground. I can't leave."

I nodded, not quite sure what to say. Some ghosts are free-ranging and can go where they like, but most of them end up fixed in one spot. John was one of the lucky ones. He could go anywhere in Harlot Bay. Some ghosts end up trapped in a single room or tied to an object. If that object goes to the bottom of the ocean, so do they.

"We'll figure out why you're stuck here, I promise."

John tried to smile at me, but I could tell his heart wasn't in it.

"Hey, I have an idea. Could you stand up so I can take a photo of you?"

"You can take photos of ghosts?"

"I can take photos of auras. Maybe I can see yours and it can give us some useful information."

I didn't know what useful information, really; I was just trying anything to get him to cheer up. It was bad enough being dead, bad enough being a ghost, bad enough being trapped in one town for endless years, and I was the only person he got to talk to? It was rough. I mean, I'm great company if I do so say myself, but people need people, even dead people.

John stood up and clasped his hands in front of himself.

I stepped back and knelt down so I could get his full body in the picture.

"Say cheese," I said.

"Hippopotamus!" John said.

I hit the button, the flash burst out, and I took his photo.

John came over and stood beside me while I waited for the camera to process the image. As I've mentioned, it's as slow as a wet week sometimes, and right then it was being particularly slow. John got as close as possible, but he was careful not to touch me. Unlike in the movies, ghosts don't go through living things. All they do is bounce off like they're tennis balls. You ever want to get rid of a ghost? Just swipe at it.

John's photo finally appeared in the viewfinder. John wasn't in it, but his aura was. It was bright blue, almost iridescent, like the wings of a butterfly. There were deep blue lines running through it like cracks. Up on his chest, near where his heart would be, there was a red mark like a wound. Running from it were strands of deep red. They crept up his neck and encircled his head like a crown. The entire top of his head was glowing in red, the blue completely pushed away.

"Does that mean I suffered a head injury?"

"I don't know. Maybe. There's something around your heart as well. That might give me a clue for where to start looking."

John frowned and lifted his ghostly hands up to his head. He felt over his skull, checking for any wounds. Then he pulled his ghostly shirt aside and looked down at his chest. There was nothing there, no injury.

He sighed and slumped back down on the sofa, focusing his attention on the Flavorstone 3000 frying pan. The people on the screen were laying it on the train track, proving that it was the strongest frying pan in existence. The train hit it and the frying pan survived. Then they cooked an egg in it.

"That's pretty amazing," John said. He seemed to be feeling better, so I took that as my cue to get out of there.

I collected my gear, told John I would see him later, and then left. I got in the car and turned the air conditioning up to high. Because it was sitting on a flat surface, the air conditioning actually worked and kicked in. It was quite refreshing. I looked at myself in the rearview mirror for a pep talk.

"Okay, Harlow, you're going to go back to the Butter Festival to take a photo of Fusion Swan and Preston Jacobs. Maybe Zero Bend, if he is there. And then hopefully, one of those photos will tell you something."

My own dubious face in the mirror told me I didn't believe myself. What else could I do, though? Someone had killed Holt Everand, and for all I knew they might kill again. They might have seen me at the warehouse, so I had a strong incentive to discover who it was before they decided to solve the problem of the snooping reporter.

I drove back to the Butter Festival, paid again—they didn't believe that I had already been there that morning—and went in, only to find that Zero Bend was already gone. He had left an exquisite carving of an angry man holding up the head of a monster. I couldn't help noticing that the monster looked a little like Fusion Swan. *Coincidence*? I looked around, but I couldn't spot Preston Jacobs anywhere. Fusion Swan was also absent. The Butter Festival still had another half hour of carving left, and some of the other competitors were still working furiously. Glancing around, it was clear that Zero Bend was the best sculptor there.

I was in the midst of doing another lap when I looked out the door and saw Fusion Swan getting behind the wheel of an expensive car. I rushed out, but he was at the end of the street by the time I got there. I jumped into my car, prayed to the gods of mechanics, and started the engine before pulling out into the traffic and following Fusion Swan. Normally there is hardly any traffic in Harlot Bay, but perhaps because of the Butter Festival, there were tourists everywhere, and I managed to drive behind Fusion with two cars in between us. He was headed toward the rich end of town. Like most small towns, the rich had staked out their spot and then congregated there. All the houses over there were on a bit of a rise, fighting with each other for the ultimate sea view.

We only drove a few minutes before he suddenly turned onto a side street. No one was going that way, so if I followed him, the chance of him catching me was greatly increased. I decided it was worth the risk. If it got really bad, I could just take his photo and then drive away. I crept around the corner and saw that he had parked at the end of the street. I parked as well and got out of the car. I saw Fusion walk across the road and up to the front of a house that definitely didn't suit this area. Most of the houses around it were fairly well maintained. This one was looking a little run-down. The grass was overgrown and the paint was flaking. It was very much the worst house on the best street. I moved closer, camera in hand, ducking behind trees. If Fusion turned around, I didn't want him to catch me. He knocked on the door of the rundown house. A moment later, a weasely red-haired man opened the door.

The possible drug dealer. It was definitely him. The man was so ugly he looked like a weasel's face had literally been transplanted onto a human body. Standing there in full view of everyone, Fusion pulled out a roll of money from his pocket, passed it to the man, and received something in return.

Another blindingly obvious drug deal? Where were the cops when you needed them? I debated filming it, but the entire thing was over too quickly. Fusion said something to the man and then did an about-face, walking quickly back to his car. I saw him stuff a small package into his pocket.

I waited behind the tree until Fusion got to his car and drove away before running back to mine and following him. It was a short trip. We drove up the hill into the rich area of Harlot Bay. Here, the houses were more correctly called villas or mansions. Think white marble, lots of glass and a mixture of styles, some places Spanish, others Greek, and there was one that looked like a Turkish minaret.

Fusion pulled into the driveway of the luxurious three-story mansion. I parked and crept up the street, hiding behind another convenient tree just in time to see Zero Bend open the front door. Fusion greeted him. I hit the button on my camera and took the best photo I could. A moment later and they were inside.

CHAPTER FOURTEEN

I didn't hang around. One thing these rich old retired people are known for is being stickybeak busybodies. Despite the fact that most of them probably knew me by sight, they would still happily call the police and report an anonymous girl stalking the streets, probably looking to break into houses. I drove back to the office, pondering what I'd just witnessed. Clearly a drug deal. That wasn't unusual. Most of Zero Bend's stories involved drugs and alcohol. The fact that his agent was procuring them for him was about on par with what I knew about agents. I'd also discovered where Zero Bend lived. It must be a vacation rental; he was probably paying $5000 a week. All I had to do to get my interview was wait until Zero Bend was alone at his house. Then I could ask him some questions about Fusion Swan and Preston Jacobs.

I pulled up outside my office and quickly checked the photo on the small viewfinder. Zero Bend was outlined in yellow, glowing like the sun. Fusion Swan's aura was more of a sick green with streaks of red through it. I closed the viewfinder and went inside to my office so I could upload the photo to my computer and take a closer look. The TV was off and John Smith was nowhere to be seen. While I waited for my very slow computer and very slow camera to do their work, I thought about whether I should tell Sheriff Hardy what I'd seen. I knew the address of the probable drug dealer, and I could also send the police to Zero Bend's right now and they would find drugs. Would that reveal a murderer?

I wasn't really sure it was a good idea for me to visit Zero Bend, even under the guise of getting an interview. Aunt Cass had warned me about anyone who tried to get me alone. My going to visit a possible murderer just seemed like the bait putting itself in the lion's mouth. There was also the problem of Jack Bishop. I'd seen him meet with the redheaded weasel man just two days ago. Did that mean that Jack was on drugs? Was he a supplier? Could there be an innocent explanation for why someone would pay a drug dealer out on a public street and receive a package in return?

I realized I was searching for excuses. I'd been teasing Molly about the librarian and Luce about the landscaper, but the truth was I was a little jealous. As I'd said before, good men are hard to find in Harlot Bay. Most of the ones with any brains had taken those brains elsewhere. Who voluntarily decides to stay behind and live in a dying seaside town? I could see my own reflection in the computer screen. Exhibit number one right there.

My computer finally finished uploading the image, so I pushed aside my dark thoughts of accidental apartment fires and what they might mean, or people who returned to their small country towns and what *that* might mean, and focused on deciphering the auras. In a larger view, I could see that Fusion Swan's aura had touched Zero Bend's. Tendrils of green had stabbed into the gold. I shivered in my seat although the day was warm. It looked like one of those creepy nature documentaries where you see a spider eat a lizard. It's nature and wonderful and circle of life and all that, but at the same time it's creepy and gross and weird.

Did this mean that Fusion Swan was a soul sucker? Maybe that's just what auras did when two people got close together. I'd have to take a photo of Molly and Luce standing side by side before I could make a judgment.

I decided to hit the Internet once more. No throbbing soundtrack this time, just a few cups of coffee and me clicking at high speed as I read all kinds of websites.

Preston Jacobs had asked me who benefited from Holt's death. As Fusion had pointed out in the police station, the list of suspects were the competitors on the Butter Festival flyer. Any one of them would benefit from a top competitor being knocked out. Although after seeing Zero Bend's sculpture, it seemed that they'd clearly killed the wrong man.

I dug into Fusion Swan and his business, the Swan Agency, and very quickly discovered that he represented many crazy people. He's actually somewhat known for representing the crazed and drug affected. Some of his clients had even died in the past. I found a famous singer who died by drowning in his own pool after too much alcohol, a child actor on the rebound trail seeking to make good before he hung himself, and a few other artists and musicians who had all died in tragic ways. It was very clear by reading through all the sites that much of the material had come directly from the Swan Agency. There was just something about the way it was written—it so closely resembled the press releases that had been emailed to me by the agency.

You could almost see the pattern spread out over time. Always the same deal: the struggle, the fight, the breakup, going to rehab, the resurrection, the fall, the destruction, the tragic death, the memorial. It was almost as if it was stage-managed, with every step along the way twisted to maximize publicity.

Fusion Swan was rich. He clearly benefited from Holt's death and was making out like crazy representing all that crazy.

I opened a new file up my computer and then sort of stared at nothing while I let all the information swirl around in my mind. There was definitely a story there. I didn't know who the murderer was, but there was certainly a story about greed, drugs and the untimely deaths of celebrities. There was definitely a story about Fusion Swan also. Had no one noticed his clients dying and how he made much hay out of the fact? I mean, it wasn't like he was killing them every month or anything like that, but there was a clear pattern. On the other hand, when you represent people who have problems, it's probably not unusual that some of them die.

I left my blank document and went back to the Internet to look up Preston Jacobs. His was a much lighter story. A North Carolina boy who had grown up on the seaside. His parents had moved around when he was a kid. He'd lived in Harlot Bay back when he was a teenager. Instead of going to college, he'd used money he'd won in a surfing competition to start a sandcastle-building-product company. He'd started with shaped buckets that made castles. It seemed like one of those dumb ideas that clearly hadn't been. He'd started manufacturing sandcastle buckets and equipment, and it had taken off like crazy. Everywhere there was a beach, there was a Preston Jacobs bucket. At some point, he'd gotten involved with the sculpting world and started sponsoring competitions and giving out prizes and scholarships. His business had expanded and he'd started manufacturing high-end sculpting tools.

He'd escaped Harlot Bay and returned successful. I suddenly felt the stark contrast between us. I'd escaped and had my own story cut abruptly short. I always had the idea that I would leave Harlot Bay, go to college, work in a business, maybe start my own, and then at some point, something good would happen. I knew I might be lost for a long time, not quite sure where I was going, but I'd always been sure I would end up somewhere good. Turns out that where I'd been going was to burn down an apartment building and then return home to recover.

I let those dark thoughts sink in and countered them with my usual responses. My family is here. I love my family even if they annoy me. There is a magical convergence on Harlot Bay and it keeps me grounded, makes me feel good. When I was away I was disconnected from who I truly am, a Slip witch. It was no wonder things went bad. You can only lie to yourself for so long before the cracks become crevices, the crevices become canyons, and the whole thing falls apart. I let the thoughts come and go and then dug into the deaths on the butter-carving circuit. I found a few; one of them was even a former client of Fusion Swan. But there was nothing to tie it back to butter carving or anyone involved with it in any meaningful way. There had been deaths at previous competitions that Preston Jacobs had sponsored, and in those cases they'd found the perpetrators. One was a man who murdered a carver because he thought he was having an affair with his girlfriend. In another, a woman died after being injected with poison. The woman who murdered her proclaimed her innocence, but they'd clearly been romantic rivals for another woman's affection.

I went back to my document and started typing. I listed a few random points—deaths on the butter-carving circuit, an agent who represented the drug affected and drunks, the money, the prestige and the greed. Holt Everand had been the most recent in a long line of people to die in strange circumstances. At first, all I had was pieces and I couldn't see the connections. It was like I was standing up on the Harlot Bay Lighthouse and the entire town was covered in fog. At first I could see only a few lights here and there, but eventually the fog cleared away and I could see one street and then another. Soon the patches of dark vanished and I found myself with an article. It didn't accuse anyone of anything—that was important. I didn't actually have any evidence that Fusion Swan had killed anyone. For all I knew, he was just a vulture who feasted on the untimely deaths of his clients.

I read through the article a few times, making sure it was fair, accurate, and factual. I didn't want to get sued. I wanted to be able to report on the untimely deaths of sculptors and the money to be made from representing those with problems. I was pondering whether to publish it that moment or wait a day to see how I felt the next morning when I heard a thumping of feet coming up the stairs. A moment later, Jack appeared in the doorway.

"Harlow Torrent. Hard at work after jumping in a fountain."

Oh, I'd forgotten that he had been at the Butter Festival. How much had he seen?

"I got a little hot. Had to cool off."

"Hot? What caused your temperature to rise?" Jack stepped into the office and gave me a look that was very much that of a scoundrel. I stood up from my computer, took a step back and crossed my arms. He was handsome, yes, and he had a grin that was making butterflies jump around my stomach. And yes, he even had some stubble that would be very nice to run my fingers across. But he was a tourist. This is how tourists always appear—sexy, mysterious and *transient*.

"Can I help you with something?"

"You can—" Jack looked at my screen. He saw that I'd left

some windows open about Preston Jacobs, the Butter Festival, and some deaths.

"Ah, so you're looking into Preston Jacobs? What do you think about all the deaths?"

I walked over to my laptop and closed it.

"I'm more interested in Mr. Fusion Swan at the moment, actually. He represents a lot of people who have died in a lot of unfortunate ways. They often have problems with alcohol . . . and drugs."

"Really? Do you think he and Preston Jacobs are good friends? Could they be working together?"

He'd taken a step toward me, and I could smell some sort of aftershave. Or maybe it was just him. Something warm, some hint of spice that I couldn't quite place. Oh no, what had Aunt Cass asked me? Had I smelled cinnamon? I took in a breath through my nose. But it wasn't cinnamon. It was just . . . male. Male with stubble and those eyes verging on blue and green, a male who knows he's a little bit gorgeous and uses that to his advantage.

"What's your interest, exactly? Are you a reporter?"

"You should come out with me."

The butterflies in my stomach started flitting like crazy.

"You're a tourist," I managed to say without my voice squeaking at all.

"You should come out with me, and we can discover whether you and I are good together."

The butterflies turned into hippopotamuses stomping their way around my body. I took a breath—I could still smell his aftershave or whatever that was—and tried to calm myself.

I shook my head. He was very persistent, but I knew just how to get rid of him.

"Okay, fine. If you're still here in two weeks, you can take me out on a date."

Jack stepped forward and held out his hand. I shook it, feeling the tiny rough patches on his skin.

"It's a deal."

He smiled at me and then turned back toward the door.

"You should know something, though: you're a tourist. I live here in Harlot Bay. So there's not ever going to be a *you and me*."

Jack rubbed his stubble, and I found myself suddenly focused on his hands. Strong, rough.

"No," he said and walked away, heading to the door.

"What? What do you mean, *no?*"

He stopped in the door and looked back.

"I know you like me. If we go out, you're going to like me even more. Then what? You're going to stick with this whole you're-a-tourist-I-don't-date-tourists bit? I don't think so."

I crossed my arms again, realized I was pushing my cleavage up, and then dropped them to my sides.

"I can take back that date."

"You shook on it. I'd be very surprised if a North Carolina girl would break a deal. Two weeks."

He smiled at me and then was gone down the stairs.

I rushed to the window and saw him walking off down the street. He glanced back up at me and grinned to himself when he caught my eye.

Then he turned a corner and was gone.

I found myself overheating again, and this time it had nothing to do with any sort of magical immune response.

CHAPTER FIFTEEN

I was working through a whole lot of complicated emotions—ranging from *just kiss Jack* to *cancel that date* to *what on earth were you thinking?*—when Mom called.

As usual, she was already talking when I answered the phone. "... can't put it over there. Tell them to take it around the back."

"Hello?"

"Oh, Harlow, good, you finally answered. I need you to come to the bakery to collect some food to take home. Your cat is here too. I found him in the pizza oven again. Did you talk to him?"

I heard Adams in the background saying, *No, I wasn't.*

"Can't you guys bring it home? I'm sort of working here."

"No, Freya and I are going straight to a business seminar after work and Ro has yoga. I need you to come to the Big Pie and pick up the food and your cat as soon as possible, please."

"Okay, fine, I'll come now."

I checked the time and saw that it was already quite late. Between the therapy session with John, following Fusion

Swan through the town, witnessing a drug deal, following him to Zero Bend's house, coming back here, researching and writing an article, and then having Jack visit me, the day had vanished. I took one more look at my article and decided I'd wait a day or two. Maybe I could find out some more information. At least that's what I told myself. The truth is that most of the time the *Harlot Bay Reader* consists of puff piece reporting on new shops opening, parks being revitalized, and houses being repainted. Apart from Holt Everand's murder, this was probably the first time I'd really written anything of substance, and I was a little nervous about letting it out to meet the world.

I locked up and then drove over to the Big Pie Bakery. It's only four streets away. Big Pie is a moderate-size cafe/bakery with chairs outside for sidewalk dining. When I was within two streets of it, I smelled the delicious food. Some days it was cinnamon sugar drifting over this town in a cloud, sweet and delicious. Other days you could smell crusty bread, fresh from the oven. Sometimes it was pizza.

At this time of day the cafe was mostly empty. There were a few tourists eating snacks or donuts and drinking coffee. In another hour the bakery would close. I pulled up around the rear and went in the back entrance to find my mother and two aunts having a very serious conversation about paint colors.

"Rustic orange gives a warm, comforting feel. We're restoring the mansion, but we're not going to be turning it into a palace. We don't want people to be scared away," Mom said.

"No, the blue is more inviting," Freya said. She was kneading dough, and I'm not sure she'd realized that it had probably had enough kneading by now.

Ro turned toward me.

"I think we need to go with bright colors. Make ourselves

stand out. Everyone else in town already uses the same style of paint. We need to be different. What do you think?"

I put up my hands.

"I have no opinion on the matter. I'm only here to pick up a cat and whatever baked goods you want to give me."

"Chicken," Mom muttered.

Ro pointed to a couple of boxes sitting on the bench.

"We need these taken home and put in the pantry. Not the refrigerator. I repeat, they need to go in the pantry. Okay?"

I went over to the boxes and opened one. Inside were delicious cinnamon donuts sprinkled in sugar.

"Understood. Pantry, not refrigerator."

I closed the box, but they must have seen me licking my lips.

"These are *not* for eating. If you want something else, although I don't think you should have it, there's food out front," Mom said, looking me up and down.

I took a look down at my hips and general shape. Perhaps I shouldn't have a donut.

Counterpoint: have a donut.

Decision made after that well thought-out argument, I went into the front of the bakery and snagged a cinnamon donut. I've eaten Big Pie donuts many times and I never get sick of them. The dough is light and just sweet enough. There is a slight crispness to it and the cinnamon sugar is perfectly spiced. The mothers swear they don't use magic to bake, but we've all felt it when we've been in the kitchen. It permeates the Big Pie Bakery. I went out to the kitchen to find Adams sitting next to the boxes, sniffing at them.

"And that includes cats!" Freya said.

"I was just looking," Adams said.

"Okay, buddy, come with me."

I picked up the boxes and took them out to my car. Adams followed. I put the boxes in the back and Adams sat in the front seat. I called out goodbye to my mom and aunts and then drove home.

It was kind of perfect timing that my mom and Freya were going to a business seminar tonight. That meant they wouldn't be at home to catch us sneaking out to follow Ro. I'd concocted a whole plan based around us going out and had carefully prepared the lies. Now they weren't needed.

I drove home, chatting with Adams about cat-related matters. This included topics such as: why wasn't he allowed to sleep in the pizza oven? Donuts *are* a good food for cats. Do we have any cheese at home? I told him he isn't allowed to sleep in the pizza oven because of cat hair on pizza (but I'm very clean!), donuts aren't really good for cats (but you eat them!) and yes, we have cheese, and I would get him some when we arrived home.

I pulled up at the front of the mansion and took the boxes in through the house and into the pantry. The place was empty. Mom, Freya and Ro were still at work and Aunt Cass was nowhere to be seen. She was probably off selling illegal fireworks or brewing her own liquor or something devious like that. I put the baked goods in the pantry, pondered stealing one, decided not to, and then drove down to the east wing of the house. I gave Adams some cheese and was wondering whether to tell my cousins of my plans to visit Zero Bend alone when they got home.

"Okay, quick meal and then we are ready for Ro to come home so we can follow her," Molly said immediately.

"Do you think this is a good idea?" Luce asked.

"Of course it's a good idea. You need intelligence on your enemy," Molly replied. I silently rolled my eyes behind her back. If she kept going to the library in an effort to appear smart to Oliver, she was really going to be quoting a lot of random things at us.

I told them of the good news that my mom and Freya were going directly to a business seminar in town.

We had a quick dinner—reheated burritos that we had made in bulk a couple of weeks ago and frozen. While we were eating, Ro pulled up at the house and rushed inside.

"Operation Nighthawk is a go," Molly said, peering out the front window.

"Operation Nighthawk?"

"It's important to give your strategies important-sounding names. That way people take them seriously."

"Okay, operation Very Fancy Mustache is a go." Luce giggled as we joined Molly at the window. If history was any guide, we had about ten minutes before Aunt Ro would leave. She always rushed home, had a quick shower and something to eat, and then rushed out again. As we waited, we quickly went over our plan.

"Wait till she is halfway down the hill and then we follow," Molly said.

"What if she gets away?" Luce asked.

"She won't. She always drives really slow going down that hill in the dark."

"We'll follow through town, making sure we stay far enough back that she doesn't see. Although it's not likely she will see us. We'll follow her, and she'll either drive to a yoga class or drive to a love affair. Harlow, make sure to bring your camera," Molly said.

"My camera? Isn't it getting a little serious? We're not collecting evidence for a criminal trial."

"Yes, we are. In the past, when we have accused them of anything, they've made up any kind of answer to get out of it. She can't argue her way out of a photograph of her walking into Sheriff Hardy's house."

"I don't know, is it going too far?"

Molly didn't answer me.

"There she goes," Luce said, tapping the window.

We snuck outside and into Molly's car. It's a bit smaller than mine, but also a few years newer, and it doesn't have that whole dying-on-a-hill problem. Molly drove.

We waited a minute to ensure that Ro was down the hill and then followed. As Molly had predicted, she was driving incredibly slow in the dark. We followed her through town, making sure we kept well back. It was actually quite easy thanks to the Butter Festival's extra traffic around to hide us. We followed her through the center of town, past the fountain and the town hall, and out the other side into the suburbs.

Ro definitely wasn't going to a yoga class.

"Does anyone know where Sheriff Hardy lives?" Molly asked.

"I think it's over here somewhere. Doesn't he live on a street that has the name of a tree? Like acacia? Or gum?" Luce said.

As with my pursuit of Fusion Swan earlier in the day, as soon as we got out of the main part of town, we were the only car in sight. Molly made sure to stay back, but I think it would have been pretty obvious that we were following Ro if she'd bothered to turn around.

"There, quick, she's turning," Luce said, pointing. By the time we reached the same corner and turned around it, Ro's car was gone. Molly pulled to a stop at the curb and turned off the headlights.

"Don't move," she whispered.

"Why?" I whispered back.

"She might have seen us. She stopped so she can catch us."

"Shouldn't we get out of here, then, so that doesn't happen?"

"No, that'll look even more suspicious."

"But if she catches us, won't that look suspicious?" I asked.

Right that moment there was an enormous thud from the trunk of the car. We all screamed and turned around, but there was no one there.

"What was that?" Luce said. She reached under the front seat where Molly was sitting and pulled out a short baseball bat.

"What's that for?"

"In case there's some monster out there about to get us. It could be the soul sucker."

I hadn't thought of that. Although, what were the chances? We're driving around following our aunt and the soul sucker just happens to stumble across us?

There was another thud from the trunk.

"Okay, we have to get out and see what that is. We're witches; we can do this," I said.

"Or we could just drive away," Molly said.

"What if the soul sucker is in the trunk? Then we take it home and there's just the three of us a mile from town."

This was getting really bad. If we kept talking, we were going to scare ourselves stupid. I jumped out of the car.

"Let's go."

Molly and Luce reluctantly followed. Molly forced Luce out in front of her, holding the bat. We crept around the back of the car. I was ready to cast a spell if I had to. Molly mouthed *I'm going to open it* and pointed at Luce to get into position. I stood on the other side of her so I wouldn't get hit by the bat and got ready to cast a binding spell. I could feel my heart thudding, and my breath in my lungs seemed to rasp abnormally loud. Everything around us had gone quiet and it seemed the night itself was closing in. Molly reached forward and slipped the key into the lock incredibly slowly.

A silent countdown.

3 . . . 2 . . . 1 . . .

The trunk sprung open and the interior light glared out. Something rose up like a viper.

"Argh!" Luce shouted with her eyes closed and swung like crazy.

There was a flash of light and the bat broke apart in her hands.

"You stop that right now."

The monster in the trunk was . . . Aunt Cass.

"Someone help me out."

I let the binding spell slip away. I held out my hand and helped Aunt Cass out of the trunk. As she climbed out, I saw that she wasn't alone in there. There was also a box that contained glass test tubes and flasks and what was clearly a Bunsen burner.

"Is that yours?" I asked.

Aunt Cass turned around and slammed the trunk shut.

"None of your business. What are you doing out here?"

"What are *we* doing here? Why were you in Molly's trunk?"

"I asked you first."

"So? We're out for a drive and that's perfectly normal. An old lady hiding in the trunk is definitely not. So you can't use the 'I asked you first' defense."

"Who are you following?"

"Aunt Ro," Luce said. "We think she's having a love affair with Sheriff Hardy."

Aunt Cass just looked at the three of us and then shook her head.

"Taking your snitching to a whole new level, I see. Now you're out collecting evidence of things people are doing."

"It's not like that. We just think that Ro and the sheriff might be together and we were curious," I said.

"It doesn't matter, Harlow. Let's just go back home," Molly said.

Aunt Cass stomped away to sit in the front seat.

"What you mean, it doesn't matter? Are you not the least bit curious what Aunt Cass was doing hiding in the trunk?"

"Does it matter? Do you think she's really going to tell us? We've lost Mom. Let's just go home before this gets any worse."

"I agree with Molly. If Ro caught us now, we would have to explain what we were doing here with Aunt Cass."

I couldn't believe what I was hearing. Normally my cousins would be first in line to ask Aunt Cass what exactly she was doing. And now they were backing away? Something was going on.

"Fine, we'll go home. But I'm going to find out what that Bunsen burner is about."

"She's not going to tell you," Luce said. We gathered the shattered pieces of baseball bat and then drove home in silence. We all knew if we started talking, the conversation would merely turn to why we were snitching and snooping. We arrived at the front door and Aunt Cass went inside without a word, taking her box of glassware with her. Then we drove down to our end of the house.

I turned on my cousins as soon as we were indoors.

"Seriously, what has gotten into the two of you? We just had an old lady in our trunk and some highly suspicious glassware which she just took inside, and there's not a single question?"

"It's our new strategy. She always lies to us anyway and so do our mothers, so why fight it? I think half the time she gets involved in things just so she could possibly get caught. It's kind of fun for her," Molly said.

I hadn't considered that, but still this was weird.

"You should stop reading those war books. You're getting all kinds of crazy ideas."

I made us all hot cocoa and tried to get a bit more out of them, but they foiled me at every turn. By the end of my drink, I was convinced there was definitely something going on. I was going to figure out what it was.

I went to bed and started listing the mysteries that had piled up on top of me: a dead sculptor, possible murderous competitors, a drug-dealing agent who was profiting from this, and Jack, who I'd seen meeting with someone I was fairly sure was a drug dealer. And now this? My aunt hiding in the trunk of a car and refusing to tell us why. It was no small wonder that I didn't go completely mad sometimes.

CHAPTER SIXTEEN

*I*n the morning I had breakfast with Luce and Molly, who were very excited about the new coffee machine being delivered today. I decided not to reopen the case of the Old Lady in the Trunk with the Mysterious Glassware for the time being. They were hiding something, but I knew I'd eventually find out what it was. Keeping secrets isn't a strong suit for the Torrent witches. After they left, I got myself ready and went down to the main house to see Aunt Cass. I wanted to show her the photos I had taken of Fusion Swan and Zero Bend together. I also needed to talk to her about what Hattie Stern had said to me about a magical immune response. But Aunt Cass was nowhere to be found. Most days she was in the lounge in her recliner watching television. The pile of books was still there, but no Aunt Cass.

"Hello? Aunt Cass, are you here?"

All I heard was my own voice echoing through the mansion.

She definitely hadn't left with my mom and aunts, and unless she had been hiding in Luce and Molly's trunk again, she had to be around somewhere. I went through the kitchen and downstairs to the lower floor. I said good morning to Grandma and then opened the flaking old door that led to the rest of the mansion. I took the flashlight that we kept hanging by the door and turned it on.

Under the house it's basically pitch dark. When our ancestors built it, they dug down at least two entire levels. That meant there was an entire level below me, and the wooden floors were old and rotting in places. I turned on my flashlight and crept through the dark, carefully testing each step. I didn't want to fall through the floor to end up in the rooms below.

I walked down a long corridor, feeling the warm dark pressing on me from all sides. You'd think I'd be scared under a mansion in the dark, but I grew up here. When we were kids, we used to come into the mansion all the time and run around through the lower floors finding all sorts of hiding places. On the next level down, there's even a hidden door behind a bookcase that swings open. There is also one of those dumbwaiters that, if it were functioning, would allow us to lift food up and down from the basement kitchen. It has been broken for decades. I passed under one or two skylights that let very thin beams of light in from above. Because this house was built pre-electricity, they used a lot of reflected and borrowed light. Subsequent generations of witches had carpeted over the skylights and plunged the rooms below into darkness.

I reached an intersection and turned left, heading roughly south. I knew Aunt Cass had a room for herself somewhere over here. We always tried to find it when we were kids but never succeeded. Eventually we'd stopped looking. I was fairly convinced she must've had a misdirection spell running, keeping it hidden from us. But after all these years, had she remembered to keep it going?

I walked down the corridor, and over the sound of my own footsteps and breath, I heard a clinking noise. Glass touching glass. Perhaps highly suspicious glassware touching other highly suspicious glassware. Convinced I was on the right track, I continued down the corridor, took another left, and saw a room at the far end with the door ajar. Light was streaming out of the doorway and the sound of someone working inside was very clear. I turned off the flashlight, the click of the button very loud in the darkness, and crept down the corridor. It's never a good idea to surprise a witch, but if Aunt Cass heard me she might slam the door and I'd never see what she was up to. I held my breath and crept up to the door. Inside I could hear Aunt Cass humming. She sounded cheerful.

"Stop snooping and just come in."

Okay, she knew I was there. I pushed open the door and stepped into the room. It was lit up by a large skylight. On three sides of the room were large wooden tables, and on each table, a lot of complicated chemistry equipment was set up. There were beakers of bubbling blue liquid, smaller ones of red and green, and a Bunsen burner boiling something in a large wide-bottomed flask.

I looked at Aunt Cass, who at that very moment was chopping a fine white powder with a credit card on an electronic kitchen scale.

"Please tell me this isn't meth."

"It's not meth. Pass me that stirring rod, the glass one over there."

I retrieved the glass stirring rod and gave it to Aunt Cass. She took the white powder over to a bubbling flask of green liquid and carefully dropped it in. After a moment the liquid turned black.

"If it's not meth, what is it?"

"It's something to help with the soul sucker. It won't be

ready for two more days, so hopefully it won't strike before then."

I looked around the room at the complicated twirls of plastic hose, bottles and titration equipment. Stick a slab in the middle of this room with a monster on it, and add someone cackling at the lightning, and you'd have your very own mad scientist laboratory. Aunt Cass saw me looking around.

"Do not snitch about this. Your mothers would lose their minds about it. I'm making a type of protective balm and that's it."

I didn't really know what to say. I knew Aunt Cass was good with potions, but I had no idea she had a setup like this. There were boxes of all kinds of equipment and bags of various unidentified powders sitting on the bench. If I had to guess, I would say some of the ingredients were super illegal.

I got my bearings, making a new area in my mind to hold the fact that my elderly aunt had a fully functioning laboratory hidden in the bottom of our house, and then pushed that aside. There was no way I'd tell anyone about it, not even Molly and Luce, who would be sure to spill the beans.

I took the photo of Fusion Swan and Zero Bend out of my bag and passed it to Aunt Cass. She looked at it for a moment and then passed it back to me.

"The tall one has power over the punk one. See how their auras are mingling? That's what domination looks like."

"The tall one is Fusion Swan, Zero Bend's agent. I'm pretty sure I saw him buying drugs yesterday and taking them over there."

"That would do it."

"Could Fusion Swan be the soul sucker?"

"Maybe. I think you'll be very lucky if you manage to see it in an aura."

"Yesterday I shook hands with Fusion Swan and Preston

Jacobs and then soon after that I started overheating like I was boiling alive. I had to practically douse myself in the fountain to cool down. I thought I was Slipping, but then Hattie Stern saw me and she said it was a magical immune response."

"Hattie was always good with things like that, so if she says that's what happened, then that's the truth."

I was a bit surprised to hear Aunt Cass agree with Hattie Stern. If they ever saw each other in public, they made very clear and obvious steps to stay out of each other's way. That included crossing to the other side of the street, leaving restaurants, and generally making it obviously known that they did not want to be anywhere near the other. Aunt Cass did not approve of Hattie Stern's push to have Harlot Bay renamed and had on many occasions called her a stuck-up prude with nothing better to do.

"So does that mean that Preston Jacobs or Fusion Swan could be the soul sucker?"

"It's highly likely. It's too bad you touched both of them yesterday. That type of response only works once."

Aunt Cass took out another sachet of powder from a drawer. This one was also a highly suspicious pure white. She measured it out on the scale and then reached under the bench and took out a packet of green herb that anyone who has watched any kind of crime show would recognize. I didn't step closer to check precisely which illegal herb it was. The less I knew the better.

"What does the balm do?"

"You smear a little on your skin. It makes you taste disgusting to the soul sucker. It can't drink your blood."

That sounded useful, but there were two days until it was ready.

"You know of any other way I can determine if Fusion or Preston is infected by a soul sucker?"

Aunt Cass shook her head.

"There are as many different types of soul sucker as there are beetles in the world. If it was one particular species, he could be poisoned by black tea. Another one makes its host permanently cold, so they will always be wearing extra clothing inappropriate to the weather. Another will make a bald man's hair grow back for the year before it gives them a fatal heart attack. All you can do is observe and see if you can pick up on anything unusual. Just make sure that neither of them gets you alone. Now get out of here. This balm is particularly tricky, and I can't have you standing there yammering at me. Don't tell anyone about this."

"My lips are sealed."

I turned to go, but a thought struck me.

"You were hiding in the trunk to protect us, weren't you?"

"Ridiculous idea."

"You're not really going to curse Molly and Luce because you know they didn't do it deliberately."

"We'll see about that. Now go!"

I left Aunt Cass in her mad scientist laboratory and walked carefully up the creaking corridors, back through the basement room, where I said goodbye to Grandma, and up through the kitchen. I'm not even sure *how* I would tell anyone about what Aunt Cass was doing.

"Hey, Mom, did you know Aunt Cass has a crazy laboratory under the house?"

Aunt Cass would curse me back to the Stone Age.

I got into my car, intending to go to work, but then I changed my mind. Sheriff Hardy had asked me for my help in a roundabout way, and so far I hadn't given him anything useful. Now I had two suspects, both of whom profited somewhat from Holt Everand's death. It wasn't much, but it might be enough.

I started my car and it shuddered and groaned like it was

going to die on me. While I waited for it to recover, I smiled and shook my head at the idea of Aunt Cass underground in her laboratory. Even witches have to keep up with the times, and ye olde cauldron had been replaced with the ye olde Bunsen burner and a warming flask, a retort stand and test tubes.

Now I had another secret to add to a very long list of information I was keeping to myself. So long as Aunt Cass didn't burn the mansion down or blow anything up, hopefully it would be okay. Although I wasn't sure quite what she would do once the mothers started having the mansion renovated.

CHAPTER SEVENTEEN

$\mathcal{I}$ drove to the police station, said good morning to Mary, and then sat in the waiting room until Sheriff Hardy came out. I followed him back to his office.

I sat down on a squeaking brown leather chair and Sheriff Hardy looked at me from across mounds of paperwork. His desk was piled high with folders and stacks of paper. I saw at least four inboxes stuffed to the gills. There were two desks against one wall, and they were piled up with assorted files that threatened to topple at any moment. He saw me looking around.

"As you can see, everything is very neat and well organized," he said, gesturing at the controlled chaos.

"It looks like my office. Any empty spot automatically attracts a piece of paper or a coffee mug or a loose pen."

"This isn't even the half of it. There's an entire warehouse of police records downtown. They're all in paper and we simply don't have the time or the money to digitize them. The only way to find anything is by using an ancient card catalog system. It's a nightmare when you're trying to look up similar crimes from the past."

"Speaking of similar crimes from the past . . ."

I told him what I'd discovered about Preston Jacobs and Fusion Swan. The deaths of all the various artists that Fusion had represented, the various crimes and murders that had occurred that centered around competitions Preston had been sponsoring, and my suspicion that somehow one of them had been involved in the murder, possibly for some sort of gain. I finished off by telling him about the red-haired weasel man and how I was fairly sure he was a drug dealer. I really wasn't sure about discussing that piece of information —having seen Jack talk to the same man just a few days ago —but I decided I couldn't keep it to myself. If he really was a drug dealer and Jack had in fact been buying drugs, then it didn't matter how handsome he was. He was trouble and not the good sort of trouble. I decided to tell Sheriff Hardy and let the chips fall where they may.

"So you say you've written an article about this? Have you published it yet?"

"No, it's still sitting on my computer. I was hoping to gather a bit more evidence. I really don't want to get sued— not that I have anything to lose, but at the moment all I'm doing is reporting on deaths and crime centered around butter carving. I can't really say anything of substance about Fusion or Preston at all."

"So what do your . . . sources . . . say about this?"

"They think it's likely that Fusion or Preston is involved in some way."

That was all I could say—I certainly couldn't tell him about soul suckers that sucked the blood and life energy out of people.

"Well, it's certainly an intriguing idea. I've already questioned Mr. Swan about his client. I have spoken briefly with Preston Jacobs at the festival. Unfortunately, unless more evidence arises, I don't really have any reason to question them again. I certainly got the feeling that Mr. Swan was pushing for me to direct my attention toward one of the Butter Festival competitors. I've questioned most of them, though, and on the whole, they have solid alibis. Some of them didn't even arrive in town until the morning when you found Mr. Everand."

"Be careful if you question them. You probably don't want to be alone."

Sheriff Hardy looked at me and then gently nodded. He had been a police officer for decades and was generally fearless, but he had enough sense to know that if a Torrent told you to be careful, you should be careful.

"I assume you're still going to be investigating Mr. Swan and Mr. Jacobs and the rest of the competitors?"

"I'm a journalist. My online newspaper doesn't run without news."

"Spoken like a true Torrent. Not a yes, not a no, and you're going to go and do something crazy anyway."

I couldn't resist.

"Do you know the Torrents well?"

"Of course. I've been a police officer for many years."

It was like playing a chess game against a solid brick wall. Sheriff Hardy stood up and I followed before realizing he had done it once again. He'd ended the meeting simply by standing up.

"Thanks for coming in. We don't have any other information on Holt Everand at the moment. They still haven't figured out that liquid in his body, and I think they're about to give up trying to find out. It's going to end up as 'unidentified biological matter' on the report. I really don't like having an unsolved murder on the books, so if you come up with any more evidence, please let me know. If you see that redheaded weasel man, stay away. I'm aware of him already.

He came to town a couple of months ago and we've already had reports from his neighbors."

I said my goodbyes and drove back to the office to construct a plan. Today was already looking like another busy day. There was another butter-carving final where I could possibly take a photo of Preston Jacobs or Fusion Swan again. I'd probably have lunch with my cousins, and then in the afternoon I had a therapy session with John Smith. In between that, I had to decide whether to publish my article, gather more evidence, or possibly take a trip out to Zero Bend's house to see if I could talk with him. I decided to hit the Butter Festival. I could investigate, and it doubled as actual work that might earn me income.

I drove back to the town hall and went inside. It was noticeably warmer than yesterday. I could immediately see why: now that they were down to eight competitors, they'd set up refrigerated glass boxes for the competitors to work in. The hall was packed with spectators who were wandering from place to place, watching the carvers at work. On a large board in the back of the hall, I saw that Zero Bend had taken first place yesterday. Only the top eight competitors had gone through, and the bottom eight had been eliminated. I looked around for Fusion or Preston, but I couldn't see them anywhere. I started wandering, checking out the butter carvers. One Asian girl, called Harmonious Twang, was carving an enormous scowling head out of butter. She was using a steel toothpick to sculpt fine lines through its hair. She was dressed sort of like Zero Bend—black and lots of punk, with ripped jeans and multiple piercings. Remembering that I was a reporter and not just snooping for some sort of spiritual leech entity, I took a photo of her. When it appeared on the viewfinder, I remembered the aura would be appearing too. Hers was purple and perfectly smooth like the butter she was sculpting. It had a clearly delineated edge like a barrier. So much for getting photographs for my website. If this strange new power didn't go away soon, I'd have to get someone to do my photography for me.

I wandered down the hall past the various other competitors. One had sculpted two kittens playing that looked so lifelike it appeared they were about to pounce at any moment. Another was sculpting a shark with bits of meat hanging from its jaws. It wasn't very good, and I wondered if they would be in the bottom four. I saw a few Ice Queens up in the stands watching over Zero Bend. The rest were gathered near his refrigerated box. They were all watching avidly, although this was a two-hour competition. I know they loved him, but seriously, could they keep up that sort of attention for that long?

Finally, I found myself outside Zero Bend's box. He had piled up all of his butter into a tall spire and was carving it away with precision strokes from the top. It was Harlot Bay's lighthouse, and it was perfect. He'd sculpted two people standing on the balcony, looking out into the distance. They couldn't have been bigger than my little finger, but each of them was rendered in exquisite detail. It was a man and a woman; he was looking out to the distance, his face distraught as though he was witnessing some great tragedy. She was half smiling; what she was seeing was a little bit funny. As I watched, he carved lines on the surface of the lighthouse. At first they looked to be nothing, but then one line touched another and he gave a swipe with a tiny metal tool in his hand, and suddenly the lines turned into cracks in the exact pattern of the ones on the real lighthouse. I stood there watching him work, marveling at his skill and precision for a while, and then I eventually remembered to take a photograph.

I lined myself up, noted the *no flash photography* sign stuck to each room, and took a photo. Today, Zero Bend's aura wasn't looking so great. Instead of being the glowing yellow it was yesterday, it was murky, with tendrils of pale green lodged in it that had made his aura go dark. I watched Zero Bend for a little longer, wondering if that was the effect drugs had on an aura. I took another photo from a different angle. In this one his aura was looking fainter, almost see-through. Was my power fading? Or was that Zero Bend?

If this new power was fading, I'd better use it quickly. Was there anyone else I wanted to photograph? I decided Aunt Cass was out of the question—it simply wasn't worth the risk. I very much preferred not having zits all over my face and enjoyed being able to walk in a straight line. Maybe I could photograph Jack Bishop, but I wasn't really sure how I'd arrange that. Every time I got near him I seemed to lose my grip on my senses. Yesterday I'd somehow agreed to a date with him. If I got stuck in a conversation with him again, who knew what would happen?

I took another few laps of the main hall, but I didn't come across Fusion Swan or Preston Jacobs. There were tourist spectators, the Ice Queens, and that was it.

It was getting close to lunch, so I put my camera away and decided to head to Traveler.

CHAPTER EIGHTEEN

The coffee machine was big, shiny and imposing. It had multiple spigots, numerous buttons, and even a red wheel that looked like something you'd use to keep a submarine door shut.

Printed in black letters across the top was Fuoco Oscuro.

"This is the coffee machine you bought?"

"I thought it was smaller. It looked smaller online," Luce said, fretting.

"It has forty-two buttons on it, and see that dial? It has twelve settings. There are three switches on the back that we think change between modes," Molly said.

"Did it come with—"

She gave me a tattered instruction manual with about a hundred pages in it. There was a coffee stain on the front. The entire thing was in Italian.

I flipped through it. Every few pages, there were pictures of a sad stick figure person suffering a variety of terrible accidents: being burned by steam, electrocuted, burned by hot water, having their hand cut off . . .

This alternated with a happy stick figure enjoying all the different types of coffee the machine made.

"Macchiato, Ristretto, Affogato . . . seems like they've covered the entire world here. Look, they have Americano." That one had a stick figure wearing an American flag t-shirt drinking from a cup and looking very happy about it.

"There are seventy-two different illustrations of coffee-man there losing limbs, eyebrows, being burned, electrocuted and generally hurt. I know, I counted," Molly said, crossing her arms.

"Have you turned it on yet?"

"Did you not hear me? We bought a death machine that just happens to make coffee on the side!"

"It might make really great coffee if we could work out how to use it," Luce said.

"And we can't send it back because we bought it second-hand. We're stuck with it."

I flicked through the manual and found coffee-man with his face a sour green and poison symbols surrounding his head.

"I can't believe Ro would suggest you buy this one. It seems crazy complicated."

Molly and Luce shuffled uncomfortably.

"What?"

"That's not the one," Luce said. "We decided to buy a coffee machine because it's a good idea, but we didn't want to give her the satisfaction, so . . ."

"The guy who sold it to us sent sacks of free beans too, so it seemed like a good deal," Molly added, pointing behind the counter. I leaned over and saw five sacks neatly lined up.

"There must be an English instruction manual somewhere. Have you looked online?"

"The Italian company that made this went into bankruptcy. I talked to this one guy online who claimed they only built six of these machines before they went down."

I looked at my cousins, who were sailing the waters between downcast and fearful.

"Oh, c'mon, it's not that bad! We'll just turn it on. See what happens."

"Your funeral," Luce said and stepped away. I looked at Molly.

"You can turn it on it you want. I happen to like my eyebrows where they are."

"Me too," Luce added.

"Chickens, the pair of you," I said and plugged in the Fuoco Oscuro.

Immediately the buttons lit up like Christmas lights and a speaker crackled to life inside the machine.

"Ciao!" a man's deep voice said.

"It talks? Great," Molly said.

"Um . . . ciao?" I replied.

Lights flickered on the front of the machine and then the voice streamed Italian at us at high speed. The buttons lit up one by one and the voice talked about each one. Or so we thought—it was in high-speed Italian. Past lasagna, pizza, calzone and ciao, we were lost.

After a few minutes, the machine said ciao again and then sat there, lights glimmering, ready and waiting.

"Argh, we're so dead," Molly moaned. "I just wanted to make a good cup of coffee."

The machine chimed and the bean hopper (I think) on top opened up. The man spoke more Italian at us.

"Seriously, it's voice-activated? How did you afford this?"

"It was heavily discounted," Luce said.

"A voice-activated, commercial-quality coffee machine was heavily discounted?"

More uncomfortable shuffling. I held my tongue until they cracked, which was about three seconds later.

"Aunt Cass loaned us some money. Not very much money! It really was heavily discounted . . . but yeah," Molly said.

"How much?"

"A few thousand. Don't worry about it."

"I'm not worried about it. You two are the ones who borrowed money from her. Where did she get a few thousand from?"

Luce shrugged. "Maybe the online business she was running?"

The machine must have picked up on something, because it suddenly beeped at us and the man inside said *"Aqua!"* quite sternly.

"Well, if you can't learn how to use it, maybe the guy who sold it to you will take mercy. See if he'll accept it returned, and he gets to keep a few hundred bucks for his trouble."

"We already went down that path," Luce said. "He hasn't replied to any of our messages, and the website is in Russian so we can't figure out who else to talk to."

"Russian?"

"They sell a lot of ex-military equipment too. I messaged someone and they offered me a rocket launcher, I think."

"Aqua! Adesso!" the machine said.

I turned the coffee machine off before the man inside could yell at us some more.

"So what are you going to do?"

Molly walked over to the sofa and slumped down on it. "What can we do? I doubt some other sucker will buy it from us. We're going to have to work out some other way to make money so we can pay Aunt Cass back."

"She might be reasonable about it," Luce offered.

Molly snorted in disbelief. Aunt Cass didn't spend much

time with reasonable, and if she did, it was generally in pursuit of getting her way somewhere else. If she was ever reasonable, it was time to get scared and watch out for the hidden punch.

"There must be someone in town who speaks Italian. Maybe they can help you."

Luce slumped down next to Molly and glumly contemplated the Fuoco Oscuro.

"Yeah, I guess," she said finally.

Molly's phone rang just as mine chimed in my pocket. A message from Mom telling me to come to dinner tonight and to "dress nice."

Oh no.

"Do we have to? What if we're busy? We could have other plans," Molly argued.

She mouthed "it's Mom" to us while we listened in.

"Yes, plans could include sitting around watching television and drinking wine! Like you guys lead such incredible lives."

Molly listened to Aunt Ro, her face tensing up. Her eyebrows were going to start twitching like Carter Wilkins's any minute now.

"Okay, okay! We'll come, get off my back already! Why do we need to dress nice?"

Aunt Ro chattered something and hung up.

Molly turned to us, worry creasing her face.

"They've invited guests to dinner tonight. I think they found the landscaper and the librarian."

"Did she say anything about Jack?"

Molly shook her head.

This was bad. Real bad.

I decided to spill the beans in a way that didn't implicate me.

"I saw some business and architecture books in the

lounge when I went to talk to Aunt Cass. I think they've been to the library."

Molly groaned and covered her face with her hands.

"And of course, two days ago they were getting the quote or whatever they were doing from William, so I'm fairly sure they found him too."

"This is crazy. I'm going to go over to that bakery right now and find out the truth," Luce said.

"No, don't do that," Molly said.

"Why not? They're meddling and I can't even go to ask a question? I swear, if you make one more *Art of War* quote, I'm going to throw something at you."

Molly swallowed, and I saw her trying to rephrase what she was about to say.

"You can't be hasty. If someone . . . pushes you into being hasty, then you're not thinking. That's how you lose . . . in life."

"That sounds like you mangling a Sun Tzu quote to me," Luce said.

"No, it's not. I made that up right now."

"They had me deliver some donuts into the pantry yesterday. You don't think . . . ?"

"If they serve magic donuts and desserts to those boys, I'm going to murder everyone," Molly said through gritted teeth.

I suddenly remembered Molly and Luce's strange behavior yesterday in defending Aunt Cass hiding in their trunk. Now I knew more of the story—Aunt Cass had loaned them a chunk of money to buy a giant coffee machine. Given that they were treading on thin ice for their apparent snitching on her, it made sense that they didn't want to annoy her any further, and the loan sealed the deal.

"You guys are too scared to confront Aunt Cass now that she's your loan shark?"

"No!" Molly said.

Behind her, I saw Luce gently nodding her head.

I wondered briefly if I should call Jack and see if the mothers had gotten to him. I rummaged in my pocket for his card. When I pulled it out, I saw it was water damaged and the number was unreadable. Stupid fountain. Stupid magical immune system. I knew he was staying at the Hardy Arms Hotel, but there was no way I was going to go walking over there to see if I could find him. Turning up at his hotel room would very much deliver the wrong signal. If he was coming tonight, I would find out and I could possibly be prepared, but if he wasn't? That would be weird.

"We just need to come up with a plan. Ideas. I need ideas, everyone." Molly stood up and started pacing the store, and Luce soon joined her.

"Do we have anything we can use against any of them?" Luce asked.

She looked at me and I shook my head. I mean, sure, I had Aunt Cass's mad scientist laboratory under the house, but there was no way I was giving that up simply to get out of a dinner. Besides, Jack might not even be there. I certainly wasn't going to get myself cursed just to save my cousins.

"Maybe Aunt Ro is seeing Sheriff Hardy?" I said.

"So we invite him to dinner? Genius!" Molly said.

"For what reason? I mean, I know him, we all do, but is inviting him to dinner a good idea?"

"We're desperate, Harlow. If they want to mess with our love lives, we have to mess with theirs. If we have some law enforcement there, maybe we can stop this whole fiasco from getting out of control."

"Or maybe Aunt Ro isn't going out with Sheriff Hardy, and it's just all weird and awkward, and then they still act crazy. They try to set us up, but now we have law enforcement watching," I said.

"I'll take weird and awkward any day of the week so long as the weird isn't focused on us," Luce said.

I crossed my arms.

"No, I'm not doing it."

"Please, you have to! It's for the good of the family. Call Sheriff Hardy and tell him to come tonight," Luce begged.

"Please, Harlow, you have to do it. He's our only hope. And if it's not this, we might have to take drastic measures," Molly said.

"And what might they be?"

"I don't know. Some sort of spell to make everyone eat faster or something, so it's over quicker? Does that sort of thing exist?"

"I don't think so."

Both of them stared at me with pleading eyes until I finally cracked.

"Okay, fine, I'll invite him. But that doesn't mean he's going to accept."

I called the police station and got through immediately.

"Sheriff Hardy," he answered.

"Hi, Sheriff, it's Harlow Torrent again."

"Did something happen? Do you have more evidence?"

"Um . . . no. This isn't about the case."

I felt myself turning crimson, as though I was asking Sheriff Hardy out on a date.

"I would like to invite you to come by for dinner tonight. Our mothers are making a big dinner and have invited some people, and we've known you for lots of years, so we thought you might like to come."

I sounded so awkward I wanted to die.

"Oh. Um . . . okay. That would be . . . good? Yes. At what time?"

"Six thirty."

"Should I bring anything? A bottle of wine, perhaps?"

"A bottle of wine would be perfect. You know where we live. See you then." I ended the call and then slumped back on the sofa, feeling like I was about to burst into flames.

"Good job. Got our first diversionary tactic in place. What else can we do?" Molly said, rubbing her hands together.

My stomach grumbled at that moment to remind me that it was lunchtime. We stopped plotting for two minutes to order toasted ham, cheese and tomato sandwiches from the deli around the corner. Because Harlot Bay is so small, they deliver. About five minutes later, Jeff the delivery boy dropped off the sandwiches, refused our tip, and went on his way.

Over lunch we continued plotting, but it seemed we'd had our one and only good idea—if it was a good idea—in bringing Sheriff Hardy to dinner. Magic was out. Given that we were up against three far more experienced witches, they'd probably be able to outmaneuver us. Generally, in these situations, we try to stir Aunt Cass up a bit and get her to direct her attention toward our mothers. But given that Luce and Molly were deep in debt to her, and also because she suspected them of snitching on her, they didn't want to.

I couldn't use what I knew either. After all, Aunt Cass was doing something to help me, even if it did look like she was brewing very illegal drugs under the house.

There was the brief idea that we could contact William and Oliver and warn them off from coming to dinner, but then we realized that wouldn't work either. Molly and Luce liked both of them, and suddenly turning down a dinner invitation they'd already accepted certainly wouldn't play well in the future.

All out of ideas, I left my cousins with their giant Italian coffee machine and made my way back to the office.

Great, just what I needed: a family dinner.

CHAPTER NINETEEN

*B*ack at my office, I realized I was late for John's therapy session. There was a fresh twenty sitting on the desk but no John. I turned on my laptop and reread my article while I waited. I had just decided to publish it when John appeared in the doorway looking very annoyed.

"Hattie Stern is such a busybody!" he declared. He walked across to the sofa and lay down on it, Freud psychology style.

I twisted the egg timer to one hour and turned to him.

"Do you know Hattie Stern?"

"I think so. I was waiting for you and I saw her walk by on the street. I know I don't like her, so I decided to follow."

This was a breakthrough of sorts. He knew Hattie Stern on sight—that might mean that *she* knew him. It also pinned him to a particular period of time. Hattie was in her late sixties, and that suddenly narrowed the time window we were looking at considerably. I just had to lead him and not get in the way.

"What did you see?"

John stood up from the sofa and started pacing the room. It was the most animated I'd ever seen him.

"She went to the council to try to get the name of the town changed again! When is she going to give that up? She's been trying to do that for . . . for . . . I don't know! I don't know exactly, but it has been a very long time. She could never help herself meddling."

"Why do you think she's a meddler?"

"I know she's a meddler the same way I know a fish is slippery or a dog barks. It's her nature. She's always been about control."

"Do you remember anything specific?"

John frowned at me as if suddenly realizing I was there. The expression of frustration and anger on his face faded away.

"I think she . . . ah, it's gone."

He sat down on the sofa and shook his head.

"What were we talking about?"

Damn, he'd lost it. But this was still great news. Maybe all I had to do was get him around Hattie Stern and see if anything else came out.

"We were talking about Hattie Stern. She runs a small lemon orchard and makes various lemon-based products."

"I don't remember her. Should I?"

"Maybe," I said.

I spent the rest of the hour talking with John about any event I could remember in the last fifty years. Part of my website is historical, and in doing that research, I've learned a bit about Harlot Bay's past. I really needed to do more on that side, though—there had been fires, murders, kidnappings and all sorts of things that I barely knew anything about.

Sadly, as usual, John came up with nothing. At the end of the session, I directed him back to Hattie Stern again, but again he couldn't remember her and, in fact, he couldn't remember me asking about her at the beginning of the session. His ghostly short-term memory was shot.

We reached the end of the session, and he thanked me and then walked through the wall to fall onto the sidewalk below. After he was gone I returned to my article again. I was fairly sure by now that I wasn't going to be sued. If I published it, perhaps I could talk to Fusion Swan or Preston Jacobs again. Maybe get more information out of them. I checked the clock and then remembered I had intended to visit Zero Bend today, but there wasn't enough time. I'd have to stake out his house tomorrow and wait for him to come home. Hopefully he'd be alone, and who knew how much of an interview I could get in before Fusion Swan possibly turned up, perhaps with a handful of drugs?

After a tiny moment of trepidation, I published the article and then sat there looking at it, hoping I hadn't done something incredibly stupid.

I was sort of sitting there staring into nothing and thinking about things when Molly turned up at the office and let herself in.

She slumped down on the sofa.

"John here?" she asked.

"Nope."

"Luce is staying back to figure out the coffee machine. That thing is mental."

She turned sideways on the sofa and put a cushion over her face.

"Wake me when it's next year," she said.

"Sure," I replied.

I had to get a few more puff pieces about the Butter Festival out of the way. I found one photograph that didn't have a person in it surrounded by a glowing aura. Unfortunately, it was of the butter shark. It didn't look very good, but it was the best image I had. As I wrote all the puff pieces, my mind drifted away to the problem of feuding sculptors, a sleazy agent, groupies, murder, graffiti . . .

It was a story about manufactured conflict that perhaps spilled over into real-life murder and missing blood. Sheriff Hardy only had part of it. The missing part was something very magical and very dangerous.

As I wrote, I realized the Butter Festival murder had really pushed me off my game. There was a lot of other news in Harlot Bay that I was missing. Yes, it was fairly boring, but, hey, small town. The city was looking at renovating the very old and rickety boardwalk and also extending it along Scarness Beach. There was a committee discussion about restoring the old lighthouse. Yet another petition was circulating from Hattie Stern to change the name of Harlot Bay to Calmwater Bay. The owner of the skating rink had applied for a permit to demolish and rebuild.

I wrote and published three articles in record time and made a few notes about all the day-to-day news. Hopefully I'd make time tomorrow to write about them. I returned to the world and saw that the day was coming to an end. It was time to stop working so we could get home to shower and dress in our "nice clothes" for the dinner tonight.

"Hey, you awake?"

"Yes, unfortunately," Molly said from under the pillow. She sat up on the sofa and looked at me with worried eyes. "If this doesn't go well tonight, I'm moving out. I swear."

I nodded at her, even though we both knew it wasn't true. Sadly, moving requires money, and that was a resource that we were all lacking. Molly's phone chimed a message. She read it and let me know that Luce was staying back at Traveler to work more on the coffee machine. She'd come home on her own.

"You don't think she's bailing, do you?"

"I hope not. Although that's not a bad idea."

I really couldn't argue with that.

CHAPTER TWENTY

*a*fter we showered and changed, we trudged up to the main house in "nice" clothes. I'd chosen a demure black dress. Okay, not *that* demure. A slight, tiny, practically hardly any, really, touch of cleavage. Molly was wearing a red dress that was far more busty than mine.

We went into the house and parked ourselves in the main lounge, just off the dining room. Our mothers were cooking up a storm in the kitchen by the sound of things.

"I swear if they put love potion in any of the food . . . ," Molly muttered.

We heard the front door bang open and Luce appeared in the lounge soon after. She was wearing a blue dress, much like Molly's, and a baseball cap.

"You guys need to help me," she hissed.

Freya walked in to the lounge and looked the three of us up and down.

"Hmm," she said. Was that good? Bad? Approval or not?

"Why are you wearing that ridiculous hat?" she asked. Luce ducked but she wasn't quick enough. Freya pulled it off her head.

Luce was missing half of her left eyebrow.

"What happened to your eyebrow?" Freya asked.

"Nothing. What? It has always been like that."

"Nothing? You left home this morning with two perfectly good eyebrows, if a little scraggly, and now you are missing half of one, and you tell me nothing happened? You didn't realize you lost half an eyebrow?"

"It's fashion," Luce sniffed. "You wouldn't understand. It's a young person thing. And they weren't scraggly!"

"You'd better not get one of those piercings that stretch your earlobes out. It's a slippery slope," Freya said, pointing at Luce.

She just rolled her eyes. Freya has a tiny obsession with watching all those shows with "Extreme" in the title. Extreme Piercings, Extreme Tattoos, Extreme Hair Styles. Luce came home with a tiny stud in her nose once and Freya acted like she'd slipped into some dark world of extreme body modification. A tiny nose stud today, two goat horns tomorrow, full-body reptile-skin tattoos the next.

Freya bustled away to the kitchen, but not before throwing a final disapproving sniff in Luce's direction.

"Coffee machine?"

"El Diablo Cafe? I've nearly worked out how to use it. Hit button sixteen at the wrong moment is all."

"Isn't that Spanish?"

Luce pointed at her half eyebrow. "Do you think I care what language it is? If I hadn't ducked at the right time, I'd be bald now."

"Okay, sorry."

"That devil machine is not going to beat me," she said, touching her remaining good eyebrow.

Aunt Cass stomped into the room, took one look at Luce, smirked, and then sat down in her recliner without a word.

"I need ideas. What can I do? This is a good enough excuse not to come to dinner, right?"

"I guess so, but then you know our mothers," I said.

"Okay, I have your backing. I'm going to the other end of the house. I'm not coming to dinner."

Just then we heard the distant sound of a car. It was definitely coming up the road toward our mansion.

"Oh no, they're coming. What can I do? They're going to see me," Luce said, panicking.

"Don't say I never help you." Aunt Cass waved her hand and muttered under her breath. We all felt the wash of magic, like a puff of air.

Luce's remaining one-point-five eyebrows drifted to the ground.

"Now just draw them on with makeup," Aunt Cass said.

Luce put her hands to her face.

"This is your solution? No eyebrows at all! ARGH!"

Right at that moment, Freya walked into the dining room and saw her daughter.

"What are you doing? Is this some new fashion? Because I don't like it. You look weird."

"She magicked off my eyebrows!" Luce said, pointing at Aunt Cass.

"So she can draw them back on. Better than dinner with half an eyebrow. If you don't like it, then do a growth spell. You can handle that."

Car lights flashed up on the front of the house. Someone was here!

"Okay, come with us," Molly said. She grabbed a nearly hyperventilating Luce and signaled me to take her other arm. We rushed out through the kitchen and into the bathroom at the back of the house. There was makeup aplenty scattered around.

Our first attempt was . . . not good.

"I look like an insane clown!" Luce squealed.

We wiped it off and tried again.

"Argh! Why am I frowning so much? That's it, I'm leaving. I'm not coming to dinner."

"The window is too small to climb out," Molly gently reminded her. The back of this area had actually been sealed off from the rest of the mansion behind it. The only way in and out was through the dining room, unless she wanted to risk traversing the under-mansion. With all the flooding in the past and rotting wood, it really wasn't safe.

"Okay, okay, okay," Luce whispered to herself. She wiped off the angry eyebrows and faced herself in the mirror.

"One of you has to do a growth spell on me."

"Not me," Molly said immediately.

"Let's try drawing them on again, it's probably safer."

"It's not working. You have to help me," Luce said.

I sighed and tried to ignore the rising apprehension. Growth spells are tricky. Cast them on a garden bed to make a single plant grow, and the entire area goes crazy. It's all too easy for a nudge to become a shove.

"Fine, I'll do it, but I accept no responsibility for the consequences."

Luce turned to face me and I took a few deep breaths to clear my mind. Well, I tried to. I could hear more than one male voice from the direction of the dining room. What if it was Jack? Could they have tracked him down too?

I couldn't focus on that now. Growth spell, slight nudge, careful. Precision.

I took another breath and felt the magic moving around me like I was standing in the ocean. Cold currents near my feet, a burst of warmth at my knees. As I connected with it, I felt the magic inside me respond. It moved up my body and then down my arm. I pushed it to my fingertip.

"Grow," I whispered, drawing my finger across the bald spots where Luce's eyebrows used to be.

I let go of the magic and felt it wisp away.

"Thanks," Luce said and touched me on the arm. She turned back to the mirror in time to see tiny hairs sprout. Within ten seconds her eyebrows were back.

We waited another ten seconds to see if they'd go crazy and keep growing, but it looked like I'd nailed it.

We heard a voice we all recognized. It was Sheriff Hardy. A moment later Aunt Freya called out to us.

"Girls? Our guests are here!"

"Everything is going to be fine, everything is going to be fine," Luce chanted. She touched her newly regrown eyebrows and smiled at us in the mirror.

"Moving out, I swear," Molly said.

With that bolstering speech, we took ourselves back through the kitchen and into the dining room.

CHAPTER TWENTY-ONE

*T*hree men were gathered at the end of the table, awkwardly making conversation. I knew Sheriff Hardy and also William the landscaper from sight. The other dark-haired man must be Oliver, Molly's librarian. He certainly didn't look like any librarian I'd ever seen. He was dressed in jeans and a casual shirt, but he had green eyes that were vivid like a beetle's wing. Like William, his black hair was somewhat shaggy. He looked more like a rock star dressing down than a librarian dressing up.

The relief on the three men's faces was evident when they saw us.

"Harlow, so good to see you," Sheriff Hardy said. Oliver smiled at Molly and William at Luce. I never actually inquired whether William and Luce had *officially* met each other. We walked over to them and Sheriff Hardy passed me a bottle of wine.

My cousins seemed to have been dumbstruck, so it fell on me to make the introductions.

"Hi, I'm Harlow."

I held out my hand to William. He shook it and smiled at me.

"I'm Will Truer. Your mothers had me quote on the land-scaping and then they invited me to dinner," he said, seeming to feel the need to give me an explanation.

I held out my hand to Oliver and he shook it.

"Oliver Spencer. Call me Ollie. Your mothers came to the library, and they wanted some information on the historical characteristics of this mansion, so they invited me to dinner."

"I'll bet they did."

"This place is amazing. I studied historical architecture. I'd love to take a tour sometime."

"I can take you!" Molly said, practically jumping in the air.

"That would be wonderful," Ollie said, smiling at her.

"Maybe after we get a few more of the renovations done. The floors are pretty dangerous down there. So very easy to stumble across things that aren't safe," I said, looking at Molly and desperately trying to transmit information with my gaze. She frowned at me.

"No, it's fine."

Either she had forgotten about our frozen-in-time grand-mother or was too overwhelmed by the cute librarian standing in front of her to think clearly. She also didn't know about Aunt Cass's mad scientist laboratory. So long as the tour didn't take place tonight, hopefully we'd be okay.

Mom came into the dining room, wiping her hands on a hand towel. She was smiling, but it vanished and was replaced with a look of concern when she saw Sheriff Hardy.

"Sheriff? Something wrong?"

I leapt in smoothly with a lie.

"Aunt Ro said we should invite him, so I did, remember?"

She recovered like a champ.

"Oh, yes, certainly. Sorry. Silly me, I did forget. How are you, Lamont?"

Lamont? How did I not know that?

"Good evening, Dalila. I brought a bottle of wine."

"Wonderful. I see almost everyone else is here. We should be ready to have dinner soon."

Almost everyone? That wasn't good news. There came a knock at the door and my heart sank as I realized the mothers had managed to pull off the perfect trifecta of love-life meddling. Sheriff Hardy opened the door.

It was Jack.

Their eyes met, and for a moment Sheriff Hardy frowned at Jack as though he knew him. Then he recovered, bringing his face back to that stone cop look he has.

"Hi, everyone, I'm Jack Bishop."

Sheriff Hardy stepped aside to let him in. We went through the introductions again and by the time we were finished, Aunt Freya had come into the room as well.

I was doing my very best not to look at Jack. It was difficult, though. He'd gone with the casual jeans and shirt look just like Ollie, and with his scruffy hair and stubble, he was looking like a rock star on his day off as well.

"Everyone is here!" Aunt Freya said, clapping her hands together. "Okay, places, everybody."

Molly, Luce and I sat together on one side of the table with Ollie, Will and Jack opposite us. She put Sheriff Hardy next to them and said that Ro would be sitting beside him. At this, Sheriff Hardy very awkwardly said, "Oh, okay."

Had we been wrong about them? Or was Sheriff Hardy incredibly good at faking that there was nothing going on?

Mom and Freya returned to the kitchen to get the food. About then, Aunt Cass emerged from the lounge and took her customary position at the head of the table.

She looked the line of men up and down with a calculated eye.

"Lamont. Good to see you."

"Cassandra," Sheriff Hardy replied.

She focused her gaze on Will.

"Your grandfather is William Truer, isn't he?"

"Yes, ma'am."

"Is he still brewing that illegal peyote wine?"

I saw Luce's eyes go wide, and a split-second look of shock crossed Sheriff Hardy's face. But Will only laughed and shook his head.

"I think he gave that up many years ago. He mainly plays bocce on the lawn and walks on the beach these days."

"And what's your name?" she said, looking at Ollie.

"Oliver Spencer. I'm the librarian of the Harlot Bay Library."

"You're the one who writes the history website about Harlot Bay and the surroundings, aren't you?"

How did Aunt Cass know there were so many different websites? The mothers really didn't bother much with computers, and my cousins were permanently connected to their phones. My laptop stayed with me. How was she getting access?

"Yes, that's right. I'm hoping to do a book one day."

He turned to Will.

"So your family are the Truers who originally bought the island?"

"Some great-great-great-grandfather way back paid five dollars to buy it from someone else who had bought it from someone else who had stolen it from someone else. We still own some land over there, but most of it has been given back now and kept wild."

"I've read about William Truer's pirate treasure—do you think it's true?"

"We don't talk about it much in my family. My grandfather went mad digging the island trying to find it, and his dad as well. It was a bit of an obsession for some of my uncles and aunts. All they've ever dug up is old bullets and rusted tin cans. I think the story of buried pirate treasure is probably just a myth."

"Shows what you know," Aunt Cass muttered. Somehow she managed to get hold of a bottle of wine. She was filling her glass to the top.

"Aunt Cass!" Luce said and then smiled at Will.

"There are a lot of things buried over on that island, treasure included, for anyone foolish enough to search."

Great. We weren't even ten minutes into dinner and already we were having problems. Before anyone else could speak, our mothers entered from the kitchen carrying dinner. It was slow-cooked roast pork belly served with root vegetables, crispy salt crackling, a ginger-garlic-chili sauce and a leafy green side salad. Mom had Sheriff Hardy's bottle of wine open and a few other bottles as well to place on the table.

"Serve yourselves, everybody," she announced.

Aunt Ro sat down beside Sheriff Hardy, and they greeted each other as though they were friends and nothing more. I couldn't believe that I could have been so wrong about them. Clearly the sheriff *had* been at the bakery and probably had just said something to them that Ro picked up, or maybe it was the other way around. That wasn't good news. I'd been hoping if there had been anything going on between them that my mom and Aunt Freya and Aunt Cass would focus on that rather than Jack, Ollie and Will.

The first few minutes of dinner consisted of everyone serving themselves and biting into their delicious meals and then groaning with pleasure. The pork belly had been slow-cooking for more than six hours. The meat simply fell apart while the crackling on top was crispy and deliciously salty. The ginger-garlic-chili sauce was homemade, sweet and vinegary at the same time, and so thick it was like jam. The leafy green salad was crisp and fresh and provided the perfect palate cleanser for the rest of it. Everyone filled the glasses with wine and dug in.

"Molly, I understand you bought a coffee machine for Traveler?" Aunt Ro said. She turned to Ollie and Will. "Molly and Luce run the Traveler tourist shop. They're just about to start selling coffees as well."

"That sounds like a good idea," Ollie said politely.

"We should be up and running in a few days once we get a bit better at making coffee," Molly said, lying through her teeth.

"I thought the Bellissimo was quite easy to use?"

"We decided not to go with that one. We got a different one."

"Does it make good coffee?" Freya asked.

"It's very advanced," Molly said. "Who wants more wine?"

"Will, how is the landscaping business going?" Mom asked.

"It's not bad. I have a lot of steady work from some of the houses on Truer Island, and I'm looking after a few of the properties over on Barnes Boulevard."

Barnes Boulevard was where Zero Bend was staying. One of the richest streets in Harlot Bay. Color me impressed.

"Do those horses on Truer Island cause you any problems? Or the gardens?"

Truer Island is home to the descendants of Spanish horses that had escaped shipwrecks. As the horses had originally been domesticated and then escaped, they were referred to as *feral* horses rather than *wild* horses. Except in all the tourist brochures about Harlot Bay, of course, because wild horses sounds lovely and feral horses sounds terrible. They roamed the rough half of the island, and every year the park service had to take some of them away to keep the population under control.

"They're not too bad. Sometimes tourists have been feeding them, so they come over and they're a bit annoying trying to get food from you. People get bitten occasionally, but most of the locals know better."

"So, Jack, what is it you do?" Mom inquired.

"Well, I used to be a police officer," he said.

Gah, what? I nearly choked on my salad.

"Really?" Sheriff Hardy said. "How long?"

"About six years. Then I decided to do something else. I'm sort of in that phase right now." He looked directly at me. "I'm really looking for something different in my life, looking to settle down."

"Do you know what you're going to do?" Freya asked as I hastily focused all my attention on my meal.

Jack bit through a piece of crackling, the crunch of it echoing through the room.

"Well, my grandfather was a carpenter and so was my dad. I actually worked with him for a while before I went to the police force. I've been thinking about taking that up again."

"How coincidental! We're planning on renovating the Torrent Mansion. Do you think you'd be interested in doing anything like that?" Aunt Freya asked, practically grinning at me.

This was getting out of control. If I didn't do something soon, Jack would be here renovating the house, Will would be doing the landscaping, and Ollie would be writing a book about its history.

I was about to say something to divert us from this line of questioning, but Jack spoke first.

"It has been a few years, so I'm probably going to start small—just a few handyman jobs, small renovations, maybe build some furniture. Once I get back into it, maybe I'll take on restoration work. It depends upon what's around."

"So are you moving to Harlot Bay?"

"I'm not sure yet. Perhaps if there is a reason to stay," Jack said.

Before I could interpret *that*, Luce kicked me under the table. I looked at her, half-expecting her eyebrows to be going crazy on her face, but all I saw was alarm and perfectly normal eyebrows. Then she pointed at the salad on her plate. The lettuce was growing. Our mothers had put tiny sprigs of herbs in the salad and they were growing too. Molly was looking at it with horror on her face. I looked at my plate and saw the herbs were growing as well, although not as fast as Luce's plate.

"Eat all your salad right now," I hissed at Luce. She quickly grabbed her growing salad and shoved it in her mouth, chewing as fast as she could. I saw our mothers looking across at her with frowns on their faces.

"Chew your food, darling," Aunt Freya said gently. I saw the salad that remained in the bowl in the center of the table was also starting to grow, so I did the only thing I could and accidentally spilled my entire glass of wine into it.

"Oh no, it's ruined, I'll have to take it away."

I grabbed the salad bowl, scooped the salad off mine and Molly's plates and threw it in there, and then rushed out of the room with my mother close on my heels.

"What is that about?" she demanded in the kitchen.

"We had to do a growth spell to get Luce's eyebrows back after Aunt Cass magicked them off. It must have an area of effect and it was making the salad grow."

"Why did Aunt Cass take her eyebrows away? What did she do to deserve that?"

"Nothing, and Aunt Cass was helping."

"Helping? Growth spells are nothing to mess around with. I'm going to have to cast a counter."

A counter is basically a spell that stops other spells in its vicinity. The more powerful the spell is, more powerful the counter needs to be.

"No, you can't do that. I cast a growth spell on Luce's *eyebrows*. It might make them disappear again."

"Okay, well, the main course is nearly over and I don't think there's anything that can grow with the dessert. Get back out there and make sure no one's lettuce is about to grow legs. Honestly, it's like you girls don't even *want* to get married."

She pushed me back out of the kitchen and into the dining room. I only barely managed to make it look like I hadn't been shoved.

The side of the table with Jack, Will and Ollie on it was fine. They were talking amongst themselves, and Aunt Ro and Sheriff Hardy were talking and laughing together.

My side of the table was decidedly different. Molly and Luce are wearing the same frozen expressions of shock trying to be disguised by fake smiles. I looked over them and then noticed that the vase of flowers sitting on the side table behind Luce had started to grow and bloom. I rushed over and deliberately knocked the vase over. It hit the carpet and luckily didn't smash. The flowers went everywhere.

"Whoops! Oh no again, I'm so clumsy. Molly, help me."

Molly jumped out of her seat like she'd been electrocuted to help me gather up the growing flowers and the vase. We got them out of the room as fast as we could and into the kitchen, where I told her in a hushed whisper that we couldn't counter the spell right now so we just had to get any plant matter out of the room that might grow.

We rushed back in and sat down to receive a trio of glares from our mothers. Jack looked at me with a bemused smile on his face. He could tell something was going on, but he wasn't quite sure what. While we were gone, the conversation had turned to the Butter Festival and then the unfortunate murder of Holt Everand. Apparently everyone had read my article and also Carter Wilkins's in the *Harlot Bay Times*.

"So, do you have any good leads?" Jack asked Sheriff Hardy.

"We get a lot of visitors to Harlot Bay and we're following up some leads," Sheriff Hardy said somewhat stiffly. His very specific response seemed oddly directed at Jack.

"Did you find out who's been vandalizing the front of the shops with paint?" Aunt Cass said, gulping down some wine.

"Again, we have a few leads."

"It was Zero Bend. He should be arrested and locked up. What is it you do all day?"

"Dessert time!" Mom announced, clapping her hands together. She rushed to the kitchen and back in record time and plunked a chilled chocolate mousse in an ornate crystal bowl on the table. She quickly served up the dessert and put in vanilla wafers I'd seen in the kitchen. There were sprigs of mint to accompany it, but she had wisely left them in the kitchen.

It was about then that Adams sauntered into the dining room. He'd been given *very* strict instructions not to speak in front of anyone not in the family. To these instructions, he'd only answered, "Maybe if I get something nice to eat, my mouth will be full and I won't be able to speak."

The little blackmailer.

There was no point locking him in any room. He could seemingly escape from anywhere. I'd hoped he might sleep through dinner. He walked under the table and vanished.

"Ollie, did you say you are writing a book? You know Harlow is a writer too," Mom said.

"I read your website. It's good."

"It's okay," I said, feeling a small, furry shape move past my legs.

"Mousse," Adams whispered from beneath me. With

everyone's gazes on me. I couldn't exactly feed the cat under the table and get away with it.

Desperate times called for desperate measures.

"Aunt Cass, you should do an interview with Ollie—she knows a lot about the town's history."

"Oh . . . yes, that would be good," Ollie said somewhat uncertainly.

"I can tell you stories about Harlot Bay that would make your toes curl," Aunt Cass said, pointing her mousse-covered spoon at him. "Do you think your book is good enough to handle the truth?"

I used this opportunity to slip Adams a bit of chocolate mousse.

Ollie laughed weakly.

"It's not really a book yet, it's more just a series of articles. I would love to get the true story."

Luce kicked me in the ankle again. This time it really hurt.

"Ow, what are you doing?" I whispered.

She indicated upwards as best she could. I glanced up at the ceiling. Oh no. There was a tendril of green creeping down around the light fixture. It was growing rapidly, stretching out and heading toward Luce. There must have been a plant in the room above us, or a seed that sprouted. There was no way we'd be able to explain this when it came drooping down to the middle of the table. Thankfully, everyone was almost finished with their chocolate mousse. Time to put into play what I had learned from Sheriff Hardy. I stood and held up my wineglass.

"Let's go outside to look at the stars and have a drink!" I said desperately.

I pulled Luce up beside me.

"Yes, let's do that right now!"

Luce grabbed a bottle of wine off the table and rushed

around to the other side. Will only managed to just get up out of his chair in time before she grabbed him and hauled him out the door. Molly rushed around and grabbed Ollie by the arm. I followed suit with Jack.

I managed to alert my mother about what was growing through the ceiling, and she rushed Sheriff Hardy out after us, quickly followed by Ro. Aunt Cass came out last, finishing her chocolate mousse. Behind them I saw the green tendril stretch down from the ceiling and hit the tabletop. I also saw Adams jump up onto the table to start licking discarded bowls before Mom shut the door.

Outside, I found myself standing next to Jack on the gravel driveway looking up at the stars. The rest of group moved across to a small veranda where there were a few chairs, and suddenly we were alone.

"That was certainly an interesting dinner," Jack remarked and sipped his wine.

"You have no idea," I said and took a gulp of mine. We stood there in silence for a minute, my heart rate slowly descending from panic at seeing the green tendril growing through the ceiling. With Luce safely away from the house, hopefully it would stop growing.

I glanced over at the house and saw that my cousins had paired up with their respective boys and were chatting and drinking wine quite calmly, like we hadn't just escaped a growing green menace inside.

"So tonight was a big setup, wasn't it?" Jack said.

"Our mothers are very determined to see us married so we can give them lots of grandchildren."

"My mother is the same. Thankfully, my sister just had some babies, so that takes the pressure off for the time being."

"Babies?"

"Twins. Boy and girl, nonidentical. They're pretty adorable."

He likes babies and works with his hands and says he used to be a cop and those eyes and that face and . . . okay, change the topic, Harlow.

"How did they find you, anyway?"

"I went into the bakery for lunch. Your Aunt Freya asked me while I was buying a sandwich."

They're just asking random men now? Wow.

My heart rate was almost back to normal by that point. Maybe this wasn't such a disaster? Then I felt a sudden push of magic, like cold wind blowing over me. Jack suddenly yawned into the back of his hand.

"Wow, it's getting late. I'd better be going. Thanks for the delicious dinner."

I looked over at my cousins and saw that Will, Ollie and Sheriff Hardy had obviously all done the same thing. They were all yawning and saying their goodbyes and thank-yous. In a minute flat they were all driving down the hill.

"Who did that?" Molly demanded, hands on her hips.

"Will and I were having a good talk!" Luce complained. I saw her lipstick was the slightest bit smudged.

"It was me. Look inside," Aunt Cass said.

We turned toward the mansion as one just as a green tendril wormed its way under the front door. Mom rushed forward and pulled the door open to reveal a new jungle where our dining room had been. The tendril had obviously kept growing. It had split into new plants and was still currently expanding. It had filled the entire dining room wall to wall and was growing out to the lounge room on one side and the rooms on the other.

She stepped back as the green tendrils came spilling down the steps.

"Anyone have any spells they need going? No? Okay. We

need to cast a counter."

"Make sure you center it on the plants only," Aunt Cass said.

I knew she was worried if we made the counter too big, it might hit her underground laboratory and ruin the soul sucker balm that she was currently brewing. For all I knew, there might be other spells in operation right now.

Mom frowned at her suspiciously but let it go. We quickly gathered in a half circle and joined hands. We focused our energy on the growing room of plants and let the magic that naturally swirled around us start to flow.

Aunt Cass was at one end of our semicircle and Aunt Freya the other. We let the energy flow in both directions down the line of witches. Both of them whispered *counter* at the same time.

Yes, magic really is that simple sometimes. Intention, power and a word. Other times it's crazy complex with precise timings, and if you get it wrong, you could die.

We could feel the growth spell sitting in the dining room. At some point it had clearly become detached from where I'd cast it to grow Luce's eyebrows back, perhaps finding a plant to bind itself to. It was like pushing on a soap bubble, except imagine that the bubble had a skin as hard as a basketball.

We pushed. For a moment we were in stasis, our counter pushing in, the growth spell trying to expand.

Then the bubble popped. The counter broke through and swamped the growth spell, snuffing it out like a candle. The expanding mass of green immediately ceased growing.

We all collectively breathed a sigh of relief. Adams came walking out of our newly formed jungle and sat down on the steps to start washing himself. I just looked at it and silently swore yet again that I would find better ways to use my magic.

This is precisely why being a Slip witch is so dangerous. I

had both Exhibit A and Exhibit B directly in front of me. Exhibit A was the small black cat giving himself a bath, quite unconcerned that he had been surrounded by a rapidly expanding jungle. No one really knows the full story—my own vague memory was of myself at four years old beside the road down the hill, sobbing my heart out with Adams in my arms. He'd been covered in blood and I think he had been hit by a car. Between one sob and the next, my very dead kitten had suddenly become very alive. It wasn't long after that he'd said his first words. Within a few weeks, Aunt Cass had found him sleeping on the bottom shelf of the oven, which at that time had been roasting chicken. No one was really quite sure how I'd done it, but Adams was seemingly indestructible and long-lived, and I'd given him the power of speech. He also seemed to be able to escape from any locked room and would often turn up in places where he was least expected. I would leave for work and he would be sleeping on the end of my bed. An hour or two later, my mother would call me and tell me to get that cat out of the bakery. Yet we never saw him walking down the hill.

Exhibit B was the now-living jungle sitting in the bottom floor of our house.

"Well, that was a nice dinner!" Aunt Ro said, smiling at all of us.

"What were the donuts you made me bring home for?" I asked.

"The donuts? We're trialing an organic preservative so we can sell them far and wide. Why, what did you think we were going to do with them?" Mom said.

"Nothing," I said hastily. "Do you need help with this?" I asked, pointing at the green tendrils.

"You girls can go to bed, we'll handle it," Mom said.

We didn't argue. I know Aunt Cass's spell had been targeted at the four men, but even for a witch as precise as

167

she was, it was possible it brushed us. It was barely eight o'clock and we were all tired. We walked back to our end of the house in silence. When we got inside I went to the kitchen to prepare hot drinks for us.

"That was a great night, all things considered," Luce said. She was smiling as much as Ro had been.

"Ollie asked me to come to an antiques show this weekend. Then we might go to dinner!" Molly said, clapping her hands and smiling.

"I'm going on a picnic with Will on Sunday!" Luce said. They squealed and hugged each other, literally jumping for joy in front of me.

When they were done celebrating they turned to me.

"So anything with you and Jack?"

"Um, no, nothing. We'll see."

I didn't want to tell them about the date I'd agreed to go on in two weeks. For all I knew, in the next few days I might find out that Jack was a drug dealer or involved in something bad. If that was the case, I would prefer the whole thing went away. Then it would be on my mother and aunts' heads that they'd invited a not-so-good man to dinner. Was he really a former policeman?

"Oh, that's okay. Maybe he's more of a slow starter," Luce said kindly.

I made us hot cocoa and we sat around chatting. Most of the discussion was about Will and Ollie and how excited my cousins were. Although neither of them would admit it, it seemed that the mothers' meddling had been a huge success. Barring, of course, the magical jungle that had suddenly grown from a single tendril in the ceiling. By the time I finished my drink, my eyes were drooping, so I took myself to bed. As I lay there drifting off to sleep, I could feel little pushes of magic coming from the main part of the house. Our mothers were clearing out the jungle.

CHAPTER TWENTY-TWO

*I*n the morning I woke up refreshed and energetic. Obviously I'd needed an early night. Today there was only one thing on my mind: talking to Zero Bend. Molly and Luce were up fairly early also, still riding the wave of excitement that comes when you have a date with someone cute coming up. They were happily chatting away and even seemed to think that their insanely complex coffee machine would be fine if they only learned how to use it.

I said my goodbyes and drove to the office. My stories were still going well, and the number of people visiting had drastically increased. As they say in the news business, *if it bleeds it leads*. After making myself a cup of coffee, I quickly got busy finishing up all my puff pieces and local general news. I managed to churn out articles about the new boardwalk and the possible lighthouse rejuvenation.

Although Harlot Bay is a dying seaside town, we aren't going down without a fight. The city was working on rejuvenating parts of the town that had fallen into disrepair. Currently, there was a discussion about demolishing the old ice-skating rink and building a new one. The owner had even applied for a demolition permit. No matter how crazy the mayor seemed, he actually had a fairly solid vision for Harlot Bay.

Soon it was midmorning, and I knew the Butter Festival carve for the day would be underway. It was down to four people, and only two would go on to compete in the Grand Finale the next day. I was sure one of them would be Zero Bend.

After publishing eight—yes, eight!—articles, I quickly packed up my bag and drove over to the Butter Festival. I didn't go in, but I looked in through the door to see that Zero Bend was still carving. I couldn't tell exactly what he was doing, but it looked like a giant human heart. I wouldn't put it past him for it to be anatomically correct. I ducked out of there, went back to my car, and quickly drove over to Barnes Boulevard. I found a spot just down from Zero Bend's vacation rental where I could watch the house and sit in the shade. With any luck, Zero Bend would finish carving soon and then come home so I could speak to him before Fusion Swan got to him.

I sat in the car with the window open, enjoying a gentle, warm breeze. The sky was blue with a few puffs of cloud, and it was a lovely, sunny day. We were heading toward summer and every day was getting warmer. Soon we would have another burst of tourists arriving as those from cold states came to visit our wonderful beaches. As I sat there in my car in the warm sun, I felt myself relaxing.

Harlot Bay has its problems, just like any small seaside town. There's not much for teenagers to do here, not many jobs, and it has various other small-town problems, but it is beautiful. The weather is lovely, if sometimes a little unsettled and out of season due to the magic in the area. Truer Island is wild, and there is a lookout you can stand on where you can see the horses running around. The mayor is doing his best to bring us back from the brink, so we always have plenty of festivals and farmers' markets and charity walks on the beach. When the tourists are here, it's busy and thriving. Everyone is happy because they're making money. When they're gone, it's peaceful and quiet and you can walk on the beach and feel like you're the only person in existence. It's wonderful and calm, and being a Slip witch, that's something I definitely need.

I was sitting there thinking about my mother and aunts' plan to renovate Torrent Mansion and turn it into a bed-and-breakfast when a sleek, shiny car pulled into Zero Bend's driveway. A slender blonde girl got out and went up to the house and let herself in. Even from a distance, I could see she was wearing designer clothes, and I would have happily bet she was a model.

I got my camera out, zoomed in on the front door and waited. About five minutes later, she came out of the house and I snapped a series of photos as she walked back to her car. She got in and drove away. It took about ten minutes this time for my camera to finally deliver the photographs because I'd taken six of them. The girl was surrounded by a glowing orange aura that had dark, jagged green spikes stuck all through it. It looked like Zero Bend's aura. Did that girl work for Fusion Swan? Was she Zero Bend's girlfriend? It seemed the evidence was mounting that Fusion Swan was possibly a soul sucker.

I spent the next ten minutes flicking through the photographs and looking at auras. I went back into the photos I'd taken yesterday at the Butter Festival. All of them had been unusable for my website, given they were stained with people's auras. I was looking at one of the photos, a carving of a baby wearing a bowler hat, and my eyes shifted focus. Jack had been standing on the other side of the glass enclosure. He was looking right at me with a slight smile on his lips. His aura was a deep green, almost emerald, and there were streaks of brown in it, dark like wood or maybe chocolate. The edge of his aura was clearly defined—almost a straight line with very little fuzzing. I wasn't sure exactly what that meant. He was closed off? Or maybe it meant he was just very well-defined? As I was looking at the photo, vaguely thinking about the color of his eyes, another car pulled into Zero Bend's driveway and the man himself got out. He was alone. He went inside.

I locked my car and walked up to the house to knock on the door.

"Mr. Bend? Harlow Torrent from the *Harlot Bay Reader*. May I speak with you?"

"Piss off!" I heard him snarl from inside. It was the first time I'd heard him speak. It was very much angry New Yorker.

"I'm the one who found Holt Everand! I need to talk to you!"

I heard footsteps inside and then Zero Bend opened the door. He was dressed in his full punk gear: black tattooed lines up his neck, multiple piercings, and giant black sunglasses with diamonds glittering on the rims.

"You're the one who found him?"

"My name is Harlow. I went to the warehouse to take photographs that morning. I need to talk to you about some of the deaths that have been happening on the carving circuit."

"You'd better come in, then," he said.

I followed him inside and closed the door behind me. The house was spectacular. There was a winding wooden staircase that went up to the second floor, lots of marble, a plush rug, and dark wood furniture. There was a bookcase set against the far wall that I'm fairly sure cost more than everything I owned put together.

"This way," Zero said. I followed him past the stairs and out into a spectacular kitchen. There was a kettle heating on the stovetop.

He turned to me. "Time for some truth, I believe."

He took off his glasses. His eyes were a startling green. Then he reached a finger in and removed two contact lenses, revealing brown eyes beneath. He slipped them into a protective case, which he stuffed in his coat pocket.

"Hi, I'm Hamish Reynard. Would you like some tea?" he asked in a flawless British accent.

I shook his offered hand and tried to work up a sentence that didn't sound completely stupid. Contenders included:

You're British?

So, British, huh?

You drink tea; you must be British?

He must have seen the look on my face, because he gave me a gentle smile and patted me on the back of the hand before going over to the kettle. It was starting to whistle.

"Don't worry, you'll get over it in a moment," he said.

I took a deep breath and let the world move into a new position. Zero Bend, crazed American punk artist, was Hamish Reynard, quiet British . . . tea-maker. Or something.

"You're British?"

Oh, well done, Harlow. Cutting-edge investigator skills there.

Hamish took the whistling kettle off the heat and poured it into two cups.

"It's important to warm the cups first," he replied.

"You're not American."

"The water needs to boil when it hits the leaves. Very important for flavor. Some argue that there are actually three teas in every brew: the initial burst, the two-minute tea, and the long soak. I prefer the simple method: boiling water, loose tea in a tea-ball, dunked a few times and then removed before too much bitterness can form. Milk?"

I managed to nod.

"I really don't understand. You're *not* American?"

Hamish handed me a cup of tea and then placed a bowl of sugar cubes on the table.

"I think sugar ruins the taste, but tea is a very democratic drink. Have it any way you like. I prefer black, no milk, no sugar," he said, sipping his.

I dropped in two cubes, stirred it and then took a sip. Oh . . . that was good. The tea burst inside me in a wave of warmth and I relaxed.

"Do you want to start again?" he asked, raising an eyebrow.

He still had his crazy dyed hair and punk outfit, but without his contacts he'd changed. Zero Bend was gone. Hamish Reynard was sitting in front of me. The tea calmed my shock and I rallied.

"So . . . you're British?"

Well done, Harlow.

"It's all an act, a game, a . . . fantasy. No one cares about Hamish Reynard, quiet sculptor. No one buys his work or experiences it. No one installs it in the lobbies of their buildings."

"So you invented Zero Bend."

Hamish smiled and sipped his tea.

"In a way. He's a mixture of two people I knew at university. Remember, a good artist copies, but a great artist steals. I stole bits of their personalities, whipped them up together, and went out into the carving circuit under my dangerous pseudonym. Voilà—suddenly I'm in demand, my work is being shown and I'm constantly working."

"All of it is an act? The fights, the breakups, the girl you apparently threw out a window?"

At this question, Hamish looked down into his drink and gave a slight frown before sighing.

"It's not *all* an act. Somewhere along the line, the drugs, drinking, sex and rock 'n' roll stopped being an act and became the way I was living. A few of the fights were staged, like the one with Holt in Tokyo. Other ones . . . it's really hard to stay calm with people sticking cameras in your face all the time. I threw Issa out the window because I was convinced she was keeping me drugged. Total insane paranoia at the time, but once she was gone and I sobered up a bit, it turned out not to be far from the truth. I certainly didn't kill Holt—we were actually friends."

All the stories I'd read online were conflicting with the quiet man in front of me. He seemed so . . . *gentle*. Impossible that he'd murdered anyone. I wondered if he knew his agent was possibly buying drugs. Did he know some model had been in his house recently? I didn't want to sound like I'd been spying on him.

"I can see you're struggling with it. Don't worry, I sometimes do too. You pretend to be someone else for long enough and then one day you become your mask. You know what I mean?"

I nodded and sipped my tea so I didn't have to say anything. Of course I knew what he meant. I'd done exactly the same thing when I'd left Harlot Bay and gone out into the world. I was no longer Harlow Torrent, Slip witch with a magical, indestructible talking cat. I was Harlow, sorta writer, college student, then dedicated employee, easygoing girlfriend. I'd played that role well, right up to the point where the magic hiding inside me had lashed out and burned an entire apartment complex down.

"It's a bit like professional wrestling. It's real wrestling, they're pushing and jumping and fighting, but it's all choreographed for entertainment. Holt and Zero were going to do a joint sculpture. A sort of bury-the-hatchet type deal. We'd make up, best of friends, and then a few months down the line we'd start feuding again. Some of the other sculptors are in on it too."

"So the competitions are all rigged?"

"No, they're real. We all want that money and prestige. But a lot of that other stuff is all for show. Including most of the fights we had."

He looked down at his cup and a tear streaked down the side of his nose.

Hmm . . . *most* of the fights. I could see that he was hiding something.

Well, hiding something *more* than secretly being an entirely different person.

"Do you know who might have killed Holt?"

"His real name was Andrew," Hamish whispered, staring at his drink.

"I found footprints in the warehouse. Were you there?"

Hamish nodded and then took a deep breath, wiping away the forming tears.

"I went down to check the butter the night before—you know, make sure the sizes, temperatures were all good. I didn't know Andrew would be there. The place was empty, which was weird, and then I heard this chanting."

Chanting? This didn't sound good.

"Did you see who it was?"

"I called out, because that's what Zero Bend would do, and they stopped. I couldn't understand what they were chanting, either. It was all echoey, didn't sound like any language I've ever heard before. I looked around and that's when I found Andrew. He was dead already. I stepped in the blood, saw the ice hammer, freaked out completely. I knew I couldn't call the police because they'd never believe it wasn't me. I bolted out of there and came back here. I was going to make an anonymous call, but . . . I don't know, I couldn't. I got drunk instead and by the time I sobered up, you'd found him."

I nearly added *and was immediately suspected of murdering him* but managed to hold back. He should have called the police. The killer might have still been in the area, but I could understand why he didn't. My first impulse had been to run, too.

I filed chanting away—I didn't really want to deal with what that might mean right then—and circled back around to whatever Hamish was concealing. I couldn't think of a better way to put it, so I just blurted it out.

"You said most of your fights were fake. You had real ones?"

"I had a girlfriend . . . it didn't last. A while later she became *his* girlfriend. We were out drinking one night and suddenly we're punching each other. Stupid."

There was no good way to change the topic to the model I'd seen earlier, so I just went for it.

"When I was waiting for you, I saw a girl come in here. She looked like a model. Tall, blonde."

"Kachina, my girlfriend. Probably picking up something. She's staying at a hotel in town."

"Do you think it's possible someone is still drugging you? I saw Fusion Swan buying drugs."

"Sorry, what?"

I put my down my cup and stood. As I did, a rush of warmth swooshed up my legs and into my head. It felt so comfortable and good. I needed to talk to the family, find out what this chanting might mean. I knew it was important, but I was starting to not care in a big way.

"I'm gonna find out who did this and you'll be okay. You need to tell the police, though," I said.

Well, that's what *I think* I said. My mouth was feeling all funny. Hamish looked at me, frowning.

"Are you okay?"

His face stretched out, his mouth opening up bigger and bigger, and before I knew it I was swimming toward the door. I burst out into the sunlight. It was singing at me.

Was I drugged?

I didn't get to answer myself. The ground turned soft like marshmallow, and everything went all melty.

CHAPTER TWENTY-THREE

*L*ights resolved themselves into my bedroom windows. I opened my eyes to find myself in bed, with Luce and Molly watching over me with concerned expressions, Adams asleep near my feet.

"Don't freak out," Luce said immediately.

"Why would I freak out?"

I felt tired and a bit sore, like I'd been running.

"It's nothing to get upset about. That's what you need to remember," Molly said.

They were really starting to freak me out now.

"What happened? What did I do?"

Molly and Luce shared a look. I knew that look well. It was the it's-bad-but-we're-going-to-try-to-soften-the-blow-although-you're-going-to-discover-the-truth-in-the-end look.

"It's not a big deal. Not many people saw," Molly said.

"Saw what!"

"Some people saw. What about that tour bus?" Luce asked.

"I'm trying to make her feel better," Molly hissed at Luce under her breath.

"Oh. Um . . . yeah, no one really saw. We found you before too much damage occurred."

Luce looked down at the floor.

"Both of you are going to get severely karate-chopped if you don't tell me what you're talking about!"

They shared another look and then Molly sighed.

"Okay . . . you were in the fountain."

"Naked," Luce added.

"Undressed. But I'm sure for only a little while. Dancing and splashing."

A memory of shaping light flashed at me. I was too hot, had to take my feathers off . . . oh no.

"Tell me precisely what happened."

"Well, the sheriff called and said you were in the fountain dancing. We drove down, rescued you and came back here. Aunt Cass gave you a potion, you went right to sleep."

"The fountain? The one in the center of the road near the town hall? That's like a ten-minute drive from here. I was naked that whole time?"

"We can't be sure *when* you took your clothes off. That's something for the police to piece together."

"The police?"

"You stole a bunch of iron nails from Ptolemy's Hardware. Told Daisy you were fighting elves. She knew something was wrong with you, so she called Sheriff Hardy. Not to arrest you—to make sure you were okay."

"When was this?"

"About four. Maybe a bit later. Why?" Molly asked.

I tried lifting my head, expecting dizziness, but none came. Whatever Aunt Cass had given me had worked.

I'd seen Zero Bend, now Hamish Reynard, near lunch. Then I was in the fountain at four. What happened in the missing hours? Who had drugged me? I couldn't believe it was Hamish. He'd mentioned he'd suspected his old girl-friend of drugging him. Was she in town at all?

"I didn't do anything else? Rob a bank, kidnap a pony?"

"Why would you kidnap a pony?" Luce asked.

"It was a figure of speech."

"You shouldn't kidnap any animal, and especially not ponies." Despite her on-again, off-again war against Adams (who was Suspect #1 in the Case of the Missing Socks and Other Miscellaneous Crimes), Luce was an animal lover through and through. Even imaginary ponies getting kidnapped was terrible.

"Not as far as we know. Stealing nails and then the naked dance. Quite a few of those tourists had cameras."

Molly had clearly given up on trying to make me feel better about it.

I pulled back and sheets and jumped out of bed . . . to discover I was wearing green stockings, a green top and a green skirt that stuck out like flower petals around my waist.

"You *may* have rented a sunflower costume at some point. You insisted on putting it back on when we got you out of the fountain. The sunflower head part is still in my car," Luce said.

I looked down at my green feet. So I had tea with Zero Bend, got drugged, rented a sunflower costume, sometime later stole some nails and finally stripped down to dance in the fountain?

I couldn't remember any of it. Everything was a confusing blur of light and sounds. I'm pretty sure I thought I was a bird at some point.

"Someone drugged me. They were probably trying to drug Zero Bend and got me by accident. We need to talk to him and get the police to his house to test all the food in his kitchen."

Molly bit her lip. Luce mimicked her.

"Seriously—there's more?"

"Zero Bend is missing and . . . someone burned his house down."

"Probably not you," Luce added quickly.

"This is the worst week of my life," I groaned into my hands.

Before I had a chance to get out of my ridiculous sunflower costume, my mother and aunts burst into the room, followed by Aunt Cass at a much calmer pace.

"Harlow, what have you been doing?" Mom cried, rushing over to grab me in a bone-crushing hug. Again I went through the wringer of hugs.

"Someone drugged me. I don't normally dance naked in fountains of my own volition."

I saw Molly and Luce both shaking their heads at me and realized too late what I'd done.

"What you mean dancing naked in the fountain? You were naked in the fountain?" Mom asked.

"Just a figure of speech. I'm not sure what I did while I was drugged. Probably not much at all."

"Why are you dressed like a plant?" Ro asked.

"I'm not. This just happens to be some green clothes I own."

"Who drugged you? Was it that boy?" Mom said.

"Jack? No, he didn't have anything to do with it. I was at Zero Bend's."

I gave a very brief and much censored version of my visit to Zero Bend. I figured I would keep the fact that he was British to myself. By the time I'd finished, my mother and two aunts were fuming.

"He drugged you! I'm going to curse him so hard he's going to regret it the rest of his life!" Mom said.

"No, don't do that! I can't be sure it was him. Just because it happened at his house . . ."

Zero Bend had told me he'd thrown his previous model girlfriend out of a third-story window into a swimming pool because he suspected that she was keeping him drugged. After she was gone, he'd sobered up. I'd seen Kachina visit his house just before Zero Bend had come home. Was it possible that *she* had drugged something in his house? Maybe the milk he put in my tea?

Giant pieces of a puzzle suddenly clunked into place. Maybe Fusion Swan was drugging Zero Bend so he would act out and do crazy things. Kachina might even be working for Fusion Swan. Given that I had no memory of what I'd done while I'd been drugged, perhaps that was what was happening to Zero Bend. Maybe he was the graffiti artist spray-painting his name all over town. I couldn't believe I hadn't asked him about it. Maybe the drugging also meant that he'd burned his own house down.

"Well, she's fine. I'm too busy for this. I'm not to be disturbed," Aunt Cass announced and left the room.

I decided to follow her lead.

"As you can see, I'm perfectly fine. Sheriff Hardy is going to investigate, and I'm sure he'll get to the bottom of it soon."

"Hmmf," Mom said.

"I'm sure Lamont will get to the bottom of it. He is very good at his job," Aunt Ro said.

"You need to stay here to rest, and that's the end of it," Mom said.

I raised my hands. "I completely agree. I'm just going to stay here and watch television and recover."

"We need to get back to the bakery. Business is suddenly booming," Aunt Freya said.

"Us too, the Butter Festival and the murder have drawn a lot of tourists," Molly added.

Within a few minutes it was just me and Adams sleeping

on the end of my bed. I changed out of the sunflower costume—Molly had brought the head in and put it behind the sofa where our mothers wouldn't see it—had a quick shower and then did exactly as I'd told them: I sat on the sofa and turned the television on. Adams came to sit beside me and soon started purring as I rubbed his ears and scratched his neck.

I'd clearly lied when I'd said Sheriff Hardy was going to get to the bottom of it. He didn't even know yet that I had been drugged. He may have suspected it, though.

I was sitting there thinking about calling the sheriff when my phone rang in my hand. It was a call from the police station.

"Hello?"

"Harlow, it's me. Part of Zero Bend's mansion burned down. One of the neighbors said that she had seen you come to visit him. Do you know anything about what might have happened?" Sheriff Hardy asked.

The moment of truth. If what I suspected was true, perhaps some of the products in the house were drugged.

"I did go there this morning, and after I had a cup of tea with Zero Bend, things started to get quite strange. I think I was drugged. I don't remember much after that, and then I woke up at home."

"I suspected as much. I know you Torrent girls are wild, but when I heard someone in a sunflower costume had picked up a display of sunglasses and carried it three blocks before dropping it off at the library, I figured something odd was happening."

Sunglasses? Library? What had I done?

"I saw Zero Bend's girlfriend go into the house and leave before he got home. Maybe she knows something about it. Yesterday, I saw Fusion Swan meeting with that red-haired weasel man and probably buying drugs."

"Okay, thanks, Harlow. I'll let you know if we find out anything else. We'll get the lab to test all the food in the house."

"Sheriff? One more question—do you know who started the fire?"

"Well, my bet is on Zero Bend at the moment, but once we found him, he gave us a good alibi. He was witnessed going into his girlfriend's hotel not long after you met with him. The hotel manager said he looked drunk, but that's the way he looks most of the time. We think the fire started *after* that. We don't really know the cause. It looks like it started in the kitchen. Maybe something was left on the stove and it took a bit of time to get out of control."

He ended the call, leaving me only feeling marginally better. So I was drugged and presumably ran away, and then sometime after that, Zero Bend came back into town to his girlfriend's hotel. Then the fire got out of control. I remembered Zero Bend making tea on the stove. Could it be as simple as leaving a kettle sitting on a gas burner?

I sat there for the next two hours or so shuffling pieces around in my mind and feeling random pain in my body. Whatever I'd been doing while I was drugged, it certainly seemed to have taken a lot of exertion.

I had dinner alone and watched TV alone. I messaged my cousins to ask when they were coming home but didn't get any response. They only stayed open late if there were enough customers. Maybe all those Butter Festival tourists and their coffee machine were keeping them busy.

At about nine o'clock, when I was in the kitchen peeling an orange and pondering whether to have an early night, a car came roaring up the road to our house. My cousins burst into the house like a tornado.

"Wehavetostopthekiller!" Molly declared.

"What?"

They'd obviously been talking about the murder and had concocted some plan, but I honestly couldn't understand a word they were saying. Molly and Luce were pacing up and down, talking at the speed of light. Imagine hummingbirds and then give those hummingbirds a sophisticated coffee machine that makes incredibly delicious but incredibly strong coffees.

"Wecan'tjustletsomeoneelsegetkilled!" Luce blurted out.

"You need to slow down, I can't understand you," I said from behind the kitchen counter.

"Noyouneedtospeedup!"

Molly blurred over to stand at the counter.

"Quick quick, give me a piece of orange oh my gosh why are you so slow right now?" Molly said, twitching.

I gave her a piece. She gulped it down and resumed high-speed pacing.

"You guys need to cut back on the coffees. One a day, *maybe*."

Luce pointed her finger at me.

"No deal, Harlow. That coffee machine is the bestthingthateverhappened to us."

"I thought you called it a death machine?"

"Bestthingever!" Luce proclaimed, turning so sharply she was almost a blur.

"The killer is going to strike again. We have a responsibility to stop them," Molly said.

"The police are working—"

"It's magical, Harlow. That means we should do something. That's what witches do."

One of Molly's favorite statements, "that's what witches do" has been invoked in the past to include drinking too much tequila on Mexican independence day, eating way too many sugar skeleton heads on Day of the Dead celebrations and . . . hmm, we really seem to celebrate a lot of Mexican stuff.

My phone rang. It was Sheriff Hardy again.

"Do you know Harmonious Twang? She's one of the competitors in the Butter Festival?"

A sinking feeling activated.

"Yes, I know of her."

"She was renting an apartment in town. Neighbors reported fighting. There are signs of a struggle and now she's missing. We found some blood in her room. We think she's been kidnapped."

"Do you think it was same person who killed Holt?"

"That's a working hypothesis. I was wondering . . ." He paused as though trying to work out how to phrase it. "I was wondering if you or your sources might have any ideas where we should look to find her?"

"We might. I'll check with them and call you back as soon as I can."

"Thanks, Harlow."

I hung up the phone and told Molly and Luce as quickly as possible what had happened. Both of them were dancing from one foot to the other like hyperactive chipmunks.

"Finding spell!" Molly said.

"We could use a photo of her. Do you have anything?" Luce said rapidly.

I didn't know where my copy of the Butter Festival flyer was, but I'd taken some photographs of Harmonious Twang yesterday. I got out my camera and clicked through the images until I found a close-up of her face. She was wearing an intense look of concentration as she carved her butter.

"We can try that, it might work," Molly said.

I put the camera down the table and we all joined hands. We focused on Harmonious's face. The magic tingled up through my legs and into my body. It raced down my arms in a golden flood.

"Find," I whispered.

Molly and Luce echoed me.

The magic swirled around the photograph, concentrated on it, and become a tiny ball of golden light. It floated up in the air and began drifting away, hopefully heading toward Harmonious Twang. It drifted through the front wall.

"Go, go, go!" I shouted.

"Shotgun," Molly said.

We ran out the front door. The golden light was drifting toward Harlot Bay. We jumped in my car and gunned it (as much as you can "gun" such a slow car).

"C'mon, we're going to lose it," Molly said. She was in the front, having called shotgun first.

We reached the top of the big hill and gained speed on the way down. The golden light was only visible to witches, so it was okay to float over Harlot Bay—well, Hattie Stern and a few others might see it, but they probably wouldn't care much. Finding spells are fairly harmless.

The golden light picked up speed as we did, as though it knew we were moving faster. There were no cars around this time of night, so I very illegally drove through a stop sign.

We kept following the light, heading across town to the gardens. They were manicured and beautiful and backed on to wild land.

We stopped outside the gardens and walked on in.

"Should have brought weapons," Luce whispered.

"It's fine, we're witches," Molly whispered back.

It was sorta true, not the witch part, but the "it's fine" part. Luce and Molly were nature witches, and if push came to shove, they could definitely figure out how to shove. Well, maybe. Sometimes nature didn't like to be told what to do. Me? I wasn't so sure. Slip witches have no control over what their powers are in many cases. I could accidentally summon up a fireball or haul in a water monster from the ocean.

The short answer was: don't rely on magic.

We crept through the dark, following the golden light that was weaving and bobbing through the trees.

I'm sure Molly and Luce could feel it too—the magic in this area was unsettled like a rough sea. It was churning, moving quickly back and forth as though simultaneously trying to escape something and being drawn toward it. We moved further into the gardens following the light. It was darker the further we went from the street. The gardens hadn't really been set up for nighttime walks, and although that was part of the plan, obviously the landscapers hadn't gotten around to installing extra lights yet.

The ball of light vanished between some trees. We kept moving in that direction when suddenly I glimpsed another ball of light in the distance. No, it wasn't light, it was *energy*.

It was glowing white, and I knew immediately that I had to be near it.

"I'll be right back!" I yelled, giving chase.

I ran through the trees swift as darkness, dodging branches and jumping fallen logs. The sound of my cousins shouting faded away, and all I could see was the ball of energy.

I sped past a tree and then suddenly I was in a clearing. Harmonious Twang was lying on the ground, barely breathing. The ball of energy I'd been following came to a rest above her. It began pulsing. Her lips parted, and a tiny white droplet of life force shimmered into existence. It rose up from her mouth and joined the ball of energy.

The ball began to contract and expand.

It shrank down as small as a marble and then expanded to the size of a basketball. I felt it pushing and pulling on the magic around me. It was *breathing* in and out, a living thing.

Beneath it, Harmonious was weakening. The tiny ball of energy had been her life force, and this thing had drained it. Soon she would die.

I had to stop it!

The ball took a deep breath, pulling magic into itself and life out of Harmonious.

I thrust my hands out and the world narrowed to a single point. Just me and the ball of energy. It was going to burst, but I stopped it, holding it in place. The energy radiated outwards, burning hot like a fire. I let some of it go, releasing steam from a kettle, air from a balloon.

The rest I directed back into Harmonious, feeding her the life it had stolen.

The energy ball swelled, but I was far too strong for it. I grinned as it struggled against my grasp. It pulled one final time and then faded like a dying ember. A moment more and it winked out of existence.

Harmonious coughed on the ground and took a shuddering breath. She was alive.

I rushed over to her. She was disoriented and fell over when she tried to get up. I laid her down and called the police.

It wasn't long before flashlights appeared between the trees. Sheriff Hardy was leading his officers and my two very upset cousins. The police attended to Harmonious while my cousins ran over to me.

Molly grabbed me and squeezed me so hard it hurt. Then Luce did the same.

"Where did you go? You were gone for ages!" Luce said.

"It wasn't that long. I was here with Harmonious."

Molly pinched me.

"Ouch!"

"That's what you get for vanishing into the night!"

"I wasn't gone that long! You two have been having too much coffee and you're on hyper mode or something."

The local EMTs had arrived and connected Harmonious to a saline solution. One was holding it up in the air while the other checked her.

Sheriff Hardy came over. He nodded to my cousins.

"Good work, Harlow. I presume you found her while you and your cousins were out for a late-night stroll around the gardens."

Oh right, he was giving us the reason we were there.

"That's right. We were out for a walk and saw her through the trees."

"Good, I'll have one of the officers take your statement in a minute."

He waved a young woman over—Officer Hartwell—and I recited my false statement to her. She asked me a few questions (did I see anyone, notice anything unusual) but I didn't have anything else to add. By the time we were finished, the EMTs had taken Harmonious away to the hospital.

We returned to the car and I saw that it was almost midnight. Time flies when you're casting finding spells, containing explosive balls of magical energy and bringing people back from the brink of death.

"I'll drive," Molly said.

I didn't argue. Stopping that ball of energy had really taken it out of me. I got in the passenger seat, and in the blink of an eye Molly was waking me up to walk inside the house. I must have fallen asleep.

We went in and I took myself straight to bed.

I didn't even remember my head hitting the pillow.

CHAPTER TWENTY-FOUR

*I*n the morning we were three very sad witches. I was tired and sore from whatever it was I had gotten up to yesterday while under the influence of some unknown drug. Molly and Luce had finally come down from their super-caffeinated high and were essentially zombies sitting at the breakfast counter, their faces pale and eyes red.

"Good morning," I mumbled when I went into the kitchen.

"Muh," Molly said.

"I feel like I'm gonna die," Luce groaned, her head in her hands.

I knew when coming down from a major caffeine boost that cold turkey wasn't the way to go. I made them coffees, which they drank with a grimace. Apparently my instant coffee wasn't as good as their super-duper Italian machine. It worked a little, however, and brought them halfway back to life.

I was eating breakfast when my mother and aunts came storming into the room. As usual, Aunt Cass calmly followed them and sat down on the sofa.

"I told you to stay home! I told you to watch television and that was it!"

"We were going for a midnight stroll," I said.

"Don't lie to me. You were not."

"Okay, fine. We were helping find someone who was missing. If we hadn't found them they might be dead," I pleaded.

Mom narrowed her eyes at me.

"Was that boy who died in the warehouse missing his blood?"

"Um," I said.

"I knew it!"

She turned to her sisters. "We need some phosphorus, boron, willow—"

"I've already made the balm," Aunt Cass said calmly and removed a small jar from her cardigan pocket.

"What type is it?"

"I'm not sure. But I am sure it will be over soon."

"How did you know?"

"The magic told me."

I saw my aunts roll their eyes. This was a standard Aunt Cass answer when she didn't want to tell the truth. Some mystic force told her. Uh-huh.

Mom took the jar from Aunt Cass and opened it. The balm inside was a pale yellow, the color of honeycomb. She dipped her finger in and then rubbed a spot of it on the back of my hand. The magic tingled through me as the balm dissolved into my skin. Freya and Ro did the same with their daughters, who largely stood there and took it, given that they were still coffee zombies. Then the mothers dabbed some of the balm on themselves.

"Everyone needs to stay together. We'll be catering the Grand Finale today and you two are coming to help. Harlow, you're with us as well."

"But our store—" Luce said.

Freya pointed at her daughter.

"No arguing. A soul sucker is very dangerous. The three of you gallivanting around in the gardens after dark . . . you could have been killed. You're coming with us to the carving Grand Finale."

"Harlow will come with me," Aunt Cass said. "I'll make sure she comes to the festival."

Molly and Luce groaned when they realized they were caught. Now they'd have to man a bakery table rather than recuperate in their shop and dose themselves with coffee again.

I faced another ten minutes or so of comments and complaints that I largely let wash over me. They ranged from "How can I be so reckless?" to "How could I be so foolish?" Eventually Mom, Freya and Ro gave up, gave my cousins very strict instructions to quickly get changed to come to the festival to help set up, and then they marched out the door.

When they were gone, Molly and Luce went off, complaining at the unfairness of it all, but at the same time they decided to eat food, get changed and go. It was easier to give in than to fight. Sun Tzu couldn't help now: he'd never faced three very angry witch mothers.

Soon only Aunt Cass and I were left in the house.

"Are you still seeing auras?"

"I am, but I think it's fading. Yesterday I took a photo of Zero Bend's girlfriend. But it looked very weak."

"Come with me right now to the main house and bring your camera."

I grabbed my camera and followed Aunt Cass down to the main part of the house. Adams came jogging along behind us, interested in what we were doing.

We went into the house and down the stairs to the basement, where Grandma stood frozen in time.

"Take a photo," Aunt Cass commanded.

I switched my camera on and waited a frustrating ten seconds before it came to life and I could take a photo of Grandma. Then we stood there waiting another twenty seconds until the image appeared.

Grandma had a beautiful sky-blue aura surrounding her, but it was very pale, and I knew it wasn't her aura that was weak, but the power itself. It was fading rapidly. Stretching out from her hands were thin red streaks of light that rose up and went through the ceiling above her.

"Quick, come outside. We need to find out where those red lines go!"

We raced up the stairs and outside, where I took a photo of the general landscape and waited again. The image appeared, showing the red lines coming through the front wall and up into the air like ribbons, stretching to some distant source.

"I knew it," Aunt Cass whispered.

As we looked at the photo, the lines glimmered away and vanished.

I took another photo. This time it was only the scenery: no red lines, just blue sky and green fields, the distant blue ocean and Truer Island.

"What was that?"

Aunt Cass sighed.

"April bit off more than she could chew—very much more. If we could find where the end of those ribbons went, we might be able to wake her."

"It looks like it's heading toward Truer Island to me."

"Could be the caves by the beach, underwater, across on Truer Island, or any of the houses between here and there."

"How did you know there would be an aura?"

"I didn't. I only thought of it today. Must be getting old."

Okay, so there was a murderous soul sucker roaming

Harlot Bay, and that didn't scare me as much as Aunt Cass admitting she was getting old. What was happening?

"Keep this to yourself. We need to go to the Butter Festival now."

As we started to walk back, Aunt Cass asked me what I'd seen last night.

"It was ball of light."

"A small one, like a marble?"

"Uh, yeah. How did you know that?"

"There are a few entities in the same family who follow that pattern. This one is called a morchint. They make a deal with a human—usually promising wealth and power—and latch on as a parasite. The human host has to kill to feed the parasite. Only a few at first, but then it becomes hungrier. This can go on for decades. It feeds until it releases a tiny ball of energy that will often explode."

"What was it?"

"An egg. Or a test egg, really. The first one isn't anything. It'll explode, maybe cause some harm, but nothing else. It's the big one you need to watch out for. Within a day of the test egg it'll feed again, consume the host and transform into a big egg. When it explodes, it gives birth to its next form."

"Can an entity actually give you wealth and power?"

Aunt Cass snorted.

"Nope. It's a trick—the dumb host makes the deal, believes it will work, and then it *does* work."

"Like a placebo?"

I couldn't resist.

She pointed her finger at me.

"That cracking sound is the ice you're standing on. It's very thin this time of year."

"I support the small businesswoman, you know that."

"Hmmf."

I told her about finding the ball of light in the park.

"You didn't try to contain it, did you?" She waggled her finger at me.

"No . . . it exploded."

I don't know why I lied about it. Maybe because I wasn't in the mood for another lecture.

Aunt Cass visibly relaxed.

"Good. Don't try to do that. We need to discover who it has latched itself to. Morchints are devious. They love causing conflict. Betrayal and deceit are their tools. They can't help themselves but to stir things up. You can always tell a morchint because all around it is strife while it sits innocently in the midst."

That sounds like someone I know. I wisely kept that thought to myself.

"Will a finding spell work?"

Aunt Cass shook her head.

"They're hidden in their host. This one could be twenty, thirty years old and will be experienced in staying hidden. Look for anyone rich and powerful and then say *Calypso* to them."

"Um . . . *Calypso?*"

"Yes, you just need to say *Calypso* to it. If it is the morchint, it cannot help but repeat you."

"Really? That's weird."

Aunt Cass threw up her hands.

"I don't make the rules. It's a lot better than some of the other variations. One of them you can only detect by touching it with something more than two hundred years old. Do you know how hard it is to get something that is actually two hundred years old? You're running around trying to snap parts off old buildings or breaking into museums."

"A lot of the competitors are famous and rich. The sleazy agent, Fusion Swan, is rich. So is Preston Jacobs. What am I supposed to do if I find the morchint?"

"You tell your mother, aunts and me immediately. We can handle it together. Okay?"

"Sure, not a problem."

"Well, we better get moving. If you saw the light ball yesterday, then today it's going to hatch. My bet is it's going to be at the Butter Festival Grand Finale."

Aunt Cass sat on the sofa while I got changed for the day. Molly and Luce were already gone, dragging their sorry selves to the festival to help their mothers set up. I took a quick second look through some of the photos on my camera. All the auras were gone. They'd only been in the images as long as I had the power.

I drove Aunt Cass to the Butter Festival. We parked a number of streets away—they were packed with cars, and we had to walk into the festival.

There were people everywhere. It was more like a rock concert than what you'd think a butter-carving festival would attract. The Ice Queens were out in force, wearing their ridiculously skimpy outfits, cheering and screaming. The town hall was slowly filling up as people made their way inside through the narrow doors.

When we got inside, Aunt Cass told me she was going take a look around and to keep my eyes open.

In the center of the hall there are two glass cases. Each was piled high with butter. One would contain Zero Bend, the obvious favorite, and the other would contain The Slice, a short, cheerful-looking brunette in her midthirties who looked like she'd fit right in working at the bakery. Multiple food stands were set up around the perimeter of the hall. Hot dogs, ice cream, Dutch pancakes, Chinese food, Indian food, sausages and bread, and then the Big Pie Bakery. My mother and aunts were over there working furiously. Molly and Luce stood at the end collecting money and passing baked goods over the counter. Both of them were still pale.

Eventually the crowd filled the hall and the attention turned to the front. The mayor and Preston Jacobs appeared. Applause rippled across the room.

"Butter Festival!" the mayor yelled into a microphone. The crowd went nuts, cheering and jumping as though he'd just said everyone was about to get a million bucks.

"Welcome to the Grand Finale of the International Butter Carving Championships. Today, Zero Bend will take on The Slice for the chance to win this spectacular trophy and five hundred thousand dollars in prize money, supplied by Preston Jacobs and Jacobs's Sandcastles."

The crowd cheered again as Preston Jacobs took the microphone. He smiled at everyone, dazzling them with his brilliant white teeth. Could this be the man infected with the morchint? How could good health be a sign of something evil?

"Thank you, Mayor. It is my very great honor to welcome these top two athletes to the Harlot Bay Butter Festival Grand Finale. I give you Zero Bend and The Slice."

The crowd went crazy as spotlights appeared. Zero Bend and The Slice made their way through the crowd and then stepped into their respective refrigerated glass boxes. Attendants closed each box and then removed the ropes that kept the crowd at bay. People started cheering and chanting the competitors' names. I looked up in the crowd and realized The Slice had a bunch of groupies as well. These ones were all men, and they were screaming just as loud as the Ice Queens. A loud horn went off at the front of the hall. The competition had begun. I turned back to the front of the hall, but the mayor and Preston Jacobs were gone.

Damn, if Preston Jacobs was the morchint, I'd have to get close to him.

I started moving around the hall, keeping my eyes open for Preston Jacobs or Fusion Swan. I need to get close enough to them to say the word *Calypso* and see if they would repeat it back to me.

I shook my head. Magic is so crazy sometimes.

Molly and Luce spotted me and both gave sad little waves in between handing over donuts and pastries to the waiting crowd. I kept moving around as time ticked by. About half an hour into the carve, I still hadn't spotted either Preston or Fusion. Aunt Cass was nowhere to be seen either.

Just as I was wondering whether I should go up into the stands to get a better view, someone tapped me on the shoulder.

I turned around and found myself face-to-face with Fusion Swan.

"So, it's the writer who is going to be sued into poverty. You're claiming that I am deliberately profiting off the deaths of my clients? Do you understand how much trouble you're in?"

"Um . . . I didn't actually claim that you were profiting. I merely noted a pattern."

"We'll see what my lawyer has to say about it. I take my reputation very seriously, Ms. Torrent. I'm not going to allow myself to be smeared by some two-bit, seaside town, country reporter. I know you don't own much, but I'm going to take it all."

I glanced at his hand and noticed the nail was a vivid green today. Fusion Swan turned his back on me to walk away.

"*Calypso!*"

He turned around to face me and frowned.

"*Calypso?*"

"*Calypso!*" I said again.

"What is wrong with you?" he said and turned away.

"*Calypso!*" I called out to him again as he walked away.

Okay, so he's not the morchint and *I'm going to be sued down to the ground. This is just the most awesome week of my life.*

A sudden memory loomed out of nowhere. When I'd first met Fusion Swan at the police station, I'd shaken his hand and had no crazy overheating immune response. That meant . . .

Okay, I needed to find Preston Jacobs and hope it was him. If it was, then I would call Aunt Cass and the mothers and hopefully they'd be able to contain the morchint before anything bad happened.

I was looking around when I felt a push of magic from beneath my feet. It was like the tide suddenly rising up past my ankles and knees, splashing at my thighs. It was cold, freezing, almost, and gone in an instant.

I looked over at my aunts and cousins. They had all stopped in place, heedless to the people still trying to pay them to buy their baked goods. They'd felt it too. There was something beneath the town hall.

I started pushing my way through the packed crowd, heading for the stairs at the back. Like many of the buildings in Harlot Bay, the town hall had been built on top of an earlier building, so there were at least one or two levels underground. In most cases, they'd modernized them and made them into air-conditioning rooms or maintenance, or sometimes even underground parking.

I finally reached the back stairs and turned to see where my family was. They were stuck in the crowd over near their table, forcing their way through to me. There came another flood of cold magic, and I knew I couldn't wait. I rushed down the stairs and into the basement. The push of cold magic came again. It was still beneath me.

At the bottom of the stairs was an old metal door that was seriously rusted. It was bolted shut and had a warning sign on it. I quickly whispered an opening spell and the lock opened under my hand.

I opened the door and found a set of very rickety old steps facing me. They were covered in dirt, but there were clear footsteps. Someone had come down here recently.

I rushed down as quickly as I could, hoping I wouldn't fall to my death, and reached the second subfloor. There was old lighting down here—perhaps installed in the 1960s—and it lit the room in stark whites. I followed the footsteps on the ground, keeping my ears open and looking for anything around me that was out of place. I turned a corner and there she was—Kachina, Zero Bend's girlfriend, tied to a chair with a gag in her mouth. Beside her was a small wooden table, and sitting on top of it was an ice-carving hammer. From where I stood I could see it was one of Zero Bend's. It had his name carved in the handle.

"Quite a story?" Preston Jacobs said as he stepped out of the shadows.

Last time I'd been close to him, he'd looked young in that I've-had-a-lot-of-plastic-surgery kinda way. Skin tight like a drum. Fake tan. Glowing white teeth. He wasn't looking so good now. His lips were pale, cracked and dried, and there was a network of deep lines radiating out from the corners of his eyes.

"Excuse me, I'm feeling a little dehydrated," he said. He placed his hand on the back of Kachina's neck and breathed in. His pale lips flushed red. When he removed his hand, there was a smear of blood on her neck.

Supernatural evil monster stuff. Great. Why can't they ever be nice? Help old ladies and mow their lawns? It's always drinking blood and doing evil.

"You framed Zero Bend for murder."

Jacobs shrugged, an oddly graceful movement.

"Well, I sort of did. It's part of the deal."

"*Calypso,*"

"*Calypso,*" he replied.

"*Calypso, Calypso, Calypso.*"

"*Calypso, Calypso, Calypso*—stop that!"

"You didn't have to make that deal, Preston. You could have become rich on your own. The morchint is lying to you."

"It has a name? Wow. I just call it my helpful little friend."

We had only been talking a short time, but already the youth and vitality he'd sucked out of Kachina was fading. His lips were turning pale again and his skin was drying out before my very eyes. He put his hand on the back of Kachina's neck and took in another deep breath, his skin flushing pink as he sucked the blood out of her. She was already pale and white and barely breathing.

I glanced behind me, hoping I would see six very angry witches coming down to help me, but I was alone. They must still be stuck up in the crowd.

Delay, delay, delay . . .

"Morchint, can you hear me?"

Preston blinked slowly and shook his head.

"What do you want?" he slurred in a much deeper voice.

Oh crap. I hadn't planned for this. I was doing anything I could to delay whatever it was he was going to do until my family got there.

"Why do you try to frame people for murder?" I asked, desperately searching for anything that could possibly keep it talking.

But this wasn't a movie, and it was no bad guy who was going to start giving me a monologue about all the evil he had done. Preston Jacobs sniffed in my direction.

"You're one of those filth witches. I remember your stink."

With that he lunged forward, moving with unnatural speed, and grabbed my wrist. The pain was sharp and immediate, like a cold burn. Just as quickly he let go, pulling back and doubling over. He started coughing, making a deep choking noise like he was about to vomit.

My wrist was bloody where he'd grabbed me. Shimmering on the wet blood was a golden honeycomb color—the magical balm.

He stood up and spat black gunk on the floor. Then, before my very eyes, Preston Jacobs aged and dried out. Deep crevices appeared in the skin, and suddenly he looked like he was eighty. A moment later, he was one hundred, a desiccated wraith, tight skin over bones.

He started coughing and then hunched over as though he had some great pain in his stomach. He fell to the floor, huddled into a ball and then . . .

Then he split open.

His clothes ripped first, and then he broke open. There was no blood and guts, just a glimmering white marble of energy that floated up. It sucked in the last remnants of the physical form of Preston Jacobs, leaving nothing behind.

The egg.

I heard clattering behind me, the slam of the door, my mother yelling, and my aunts shouting spells. I felt the push of magic, Aunt Cass's voice sounding deeper than I'd ever heard it. The magic welled up around me, spells racing over, but it was all too late. This egg would explode and kill everyone above us. I knew instantly it would seed hundreds of new morchint eggs for miles around. It would only take in one great breath before it detonated.

The world narrowed, and my mother's frantic shouting faded away as I leapt forward with my hands out and grabbed the egg. It breathed in, taking in a gulp of the magic around us, and I felt its power. The tiny egg that I'd stopped in the park yesterday had been nothing compared to this. This was an entity that had been growing for decades, killing and sucking in life force. Now it was feeding on the magic in Harlot Bay itself.

But it was no match for a Slip witch.

I called on the magic within me and the magic around me, and it answered with a roar of power.

The egg tried to explode, but it couldn't. It was an intense heat, a fireball, a storm of pain, but it was at a distance. It couldn't burn me, couldn't hurt me. I had to keep concentrating on it. All I had to do was hold it in place and gently allow the energy to radiate away. I directed a tiny bit of it back toward Kachina, ensuring she would live. The rest I let radiate away into the air.

The power spiked higher, but I was stronger than it. I grinned to myself as the ball of pure burning fire between my hands started to falter and dwindle.

Just a moment more, just a moment more.

The egg began to collapse in on itself as I slowly released its energy so it couldn't explode. I pushed in on it, crushing it between my hands and grinning with joy at the sheer power flowing through me. Almost there.

The egg was down to a marble, the living entity inside it furiously scrabbling, trying to get away, but there was no escape.

It was snuffed out of existence and I turned around to face my family.

"I did it!"

Oh crap.

I was in the basement standing next to Grandma and . . . I was wearing an old wedding dress over the top of my clothes. I also had a party hat on top of my head.

"Did what, exactly?"

Aunt Cass emerged from the dark.

"I . . . held the energy ball. Stopped it from exploding. I saved all those people."

"We had it contained. You've been frozen like April for six weeks after you siphoned all that energy off."

Six weeks?

"Is that what happened to her? She was fighting a morchint?"

Cass whacked me in the shin with a cane.

"No! Next time listen to what I tell you. Now go upstairs and tell everyone you're back."

"Ow!"

I rubbed my shin. I'd really been down there six weeks? I looked over at the wall and saw that it was covered in photos. Me wearing a wedding dress, me wearing a hula hoop, me wearing a variety of fancy masks and different types of makeup. Obviously my cousins had had a lot of fun while I'd been frozen.

I went up the stairs with Aunt Cass climbing up behind me. When I emerged in the kitchen, my mom and two aunts were there focused on their cooking. They must have thought I was Aunt Cass, because they didn't even look around.

"Hi, everyone," I said.

Mom was cutting tomatoes. She dropped the knife, which bounced off the chopping board and fell onto the floor, narrowly missing Adams, who was waiting for any fortunate scraps to fall his way.

"Harlow!" she cried and pulled me into a hug. She crushed me against her, heedless of the tomato juice on her hands, staining what was probably her wedding dress.

"Hi, Mom," I managed to whisper from within her tight grasp.

From the dining room I heard my cousins call out my name and then their footsteps running toward the kitchen.

CHAPTER 25

"So the best you could come up with was that I was in France for six weeks?"

"What were we supposed to do? You didn't tell us that you had arranged a date with him. The poor boy just showed up at the house expecting you'd be here, and what could we say? Yes, she's here but she's frozen downstairs for some unknown length of time? I had to think on my feet," Molly said, shrugging.

"Just to get this straight: immediately after the Butter Festival, I hop on a plane and go to France for six weeks and now I'm back."

"Hey, I could have sent you to Botswana. What do you know about Botswana?"

"Botswana probably would be better than France. The could be people here in town that I'm going to lie to who have *actually* been to France or know a lot about it. You know anyone who has been to Botswana?"

"Michael Erikson. His girlfriend," Luce said, starting to count them off.

"That was when we were in high school and they were

207

exchange students. It doesn't count. Besides, they don't even live in Harlot Bay anymore."

We were back at our end of the mansion after a very emotional dinner that was alternately loving and then contained a lot of instructions on things that I was *never to do again*. Such as: never to try to contain a ball of energy ever again. I was never allowed to run off into some spooky underground death trap ever again.

It was Aunt Cass who finally told my mother and aunts to give me a break. The morchint had been destroyed, and that was the end of it.

They filled me in on what had happened while I was frozen. My mother and aunts had to cast a concealment spell on me and then shoved me over to one side of the under-ground basement. They called the police and ambulance to save Kachina. The EMTs had taken her out through the hall. Zero Bend had already finished carving (he won). He'd come rushing out of his glass container to his girlfriend's side.

My mother told Sheriff Hardy it was Preston Jacobs who had held Kachina underground, and when she finally woke up she confirmed it. He'd grabbed her very late the previous night and somehow drugged her so she couldn't wake up properly. Zero had been spending the night elsewhere medi-tating, so he didn't know she was gone. At the kidnapping news, a statewide manhunt was launched for Preston Jacobs, but of course he would never be found. The morchint had consumed him entirely.

Preston Jacobs was now the number one suspect in the death of Holt Everand. Cases in the past where people died in connection to any carving competition that Preston had sponsored were now being reviewed. There are at least two people in prison who had been framed, and hopefully they would find the evidence to clear them.

In the hospital with Kachina, Zero Bend had started to freak out, but this time they sedated him and took a blood sample. Someone eventually tested the food that he had been carrying in his bag. It had been laced with a powerful hallucinogen, and shortly after that, Fusion Swan was arrested. In the burned wreckage of Zero Bend's vacation rental, they'd found that the milk in the refrigerator had been laced with the same hallucinogen. The red-haired man was in fact a drug dealer, and Fusion Swan had been buying from him while he was in town. This news made me suddenly sad, because that meant that Jack had been buying from a drug dealer.

Molly cheered me up a little, though.

"Oh, you should hear this crazy news. Jack is actually a private investigator! You know he told us he used to work for the police? He sort of still does. He'd been tracking Preston Jacobs all across the country and around the world. A mother of a competitor who died in a carving competition hired Jack because she suspected Preston Jacobs. Isn't that crazy?"

More pieces of the puzzle suddenly fit together. So Jack wasn't buying drugs from red-haired weasel man. He was using him as a source, tracking down what was happening with Fusion Swan and Preston Jacobs. Then he'd turned up at my house for our date, and I'd stood him up because I was frozen in the basement.

Molly told me sadly that as far as they knew, Jack had left town.

That news hurt more than it should have.

Harmonious Twang had recovered well from her ordeal and left town a number of weeks ago. Zero Bend had fired Fusion Swan and then he and his girlfriend had gone into rehab.

That was everything I'd heard before I was hit with an

incredible tiredness. When you're frozen, you don't exactly sleep and it catches up with you.

Two days later, I was sitting at the dining table building myself up to going to work and looking through the dress-up photos my cousins had taken. Me as a bride, me wearing a snorkel. In all the photos was Adams, resting on my shoulder, rubbing his face against me, sleeping at my feet. He hadn't left my side the entire time.

So much had changed in just six weeks. The night before the Grand Finale, a drugged Zero Bend had graffitied his name in giant letters on Traveler's front window. My cousins hadn't found it until the next day when they returned to work. A few weeks later, he'd sent them an apology for the vandalism and a check for three thousand dollars for "cleaning costs." They'd managed to hold on to it for all of ten seconds before Aunt Cass claimed it for the coffee machine debt.

Aunt Cass had then invested that money into renovating Torrent Mansion, helping start the transformation into a bed-and-breakfast. Workmen were already at the mansion, clearing out old rooms, shoring up the floor, working from the middle outward. Grandma was downstairs with a permanent concealing spell cast on her.

My cousins were dating!

It was all very hush-hush because they didn't want to ever admit the mothers' meddling had been incredibly successful, but both of them were finding it hard to contain their joy.

I shuffled through the photos one more time. The expression on my face matched Grandma's. Whatever she was doing while she was frozen, she was happy about it. I packed them away and then went outside.

The day was warm, summer six weeks closer now. I drove to my office. My *very* dusty office.

There was a pile of twenty-dollar bills sitting on the desk, and John Smith was waiting for me on the sofa. He must have kept coming in, bringing money each time and not realizing I wasn't around.

"How are you doing?" he said.

I blew dust off my coffee mug and then sneezed. My website would surely have a layer of digital dust on it too.

"I'm good, John. Ready for therapy?"

Just then, I heard a loud banging from the ground floor and some men talking. Something heavy crashed.

I went to the door and looked down the stairwell. At the bottom was a young man trying to maneuver a very large desk in through the very narrow front door. He had shaggy black hair and when he looked up at me, he looked familiar.

"Hey," he shouted up. "I'm your new neighbor. Nice to meet you!"

"Hey," I called out and waved. The young man backed up and finally got the desk in. The man holding the other end of it stepped through the doorway and looked up at me with those eyes that bordered on blue and green.

"Hi, Harlow," Jack said.

AUTHOR NOTE

Read Treasure Witch (Torrent Witches #2) now!

Thanks for reading my book! More witch stories to come. If you'd like an email when a new book is released then you can sign up for my mailing list. I have a strict no spam policy and will only send an email when I have a new release.

I hope you enjoyed my work! If you have time, please write a review. They make all the difference to indie Authors.

In the next book Harlow finds herself tangled up in a mystery when two skeletons are dug up on Truer Island!

xx Tess

TessLake.com

Made in the USA
Columbia, SC
03 December 2021

50327863R00133